SOME FORM OF GRACE

DEE DEE CHUMLEY

Published by: 2B Publishing LLC

Cover Design by Bespoke Book Covers

Formatting by Frostbite Publishing

The characters and events portrayed in this book are fictitious. Any similarity to real persons, living or dead is coincidental and not intended by the author.

ISBN 978-0-692-94148-5

*To Robin
and to the dedicated volunteers who work so tirelessly with Exodus
House*

PREFACE

... a child stands with her nose pressed against a rusty screen and stares into a moonless, starless sky. The dark hides everything, but she knows what's beyond the window: a rickety shed draped with cobwebs, a scum-covered pond surrounded by a tangle of woods. Hot, muggy air pushes through the screen and settles on the child's goose-fleshed skin. She shudders and scrambles back to the bed she shares with two other girls. Chirps and croaks and far-off coyote yelps mingle with her bedmates' deep, steady breathing. Suddenly the tinkling of a wind chime drowns out all sounds except that of a man's raspy voice filtering through the window. "Heeeey, little girl, I know you're in there. Come out and play with me." She pulls the bed sheet over her head and curls into a ball as the man's low, mean laugh is replaced by angry shouts. And then the shouts are replaced by screams.

CHAPTER ONE

grace—*charm, attractiveness, beauty, ease of movement*
smug—*contentedly confident in one's ability, superiority, or correctness*
purgatory—*any condition or place of temporary punishment or suffering*

I SAT ACROSS FROM REGINA MADISON WITH MY HANDS TUCKED under my thighs and my head down. My eyes were glued to the stack of papers on the metal-gray table between us.

Regina leaned forward on her elbows. "So what do you think, Gracene?"

What did I think? I thought Regina's voice was as smooth and tempting as a Hershey's Kiss. And I thought if I filled out this application for Transformation Place and it was okayed, I'd be going straight from one prison to another.

On the top page, I read the words *policies, procedures, requirements*. After I chewed on them for a few seconds, they settled like cold pizza in my gut. Those were just fancy words for rules, and I'd never been too good with rules. To make matters worse, these policies and procedures were set up by a church. I'd never been too good with church, either.

A brown index finger slid down the page and stopped at something written in heavy black ink: Vision Statement.

"Pay close attention to this." Regina tapped on the page and read out loud. "'With God's grace, change is possible.'" She paused for a second. When she spoke again, her voice was softer. "We truly believe this at Transformation Place. And we have the real-life stories to prove it."

I kept my head lowered and nodded—a slow, heavy nod meant to convince Regina I was listening and giving this matter serious consideration.

In seventy-two days, I'd be released from Kate Barnard Community Corrections Center, a minimum-security facility in Oklahoma City. I'd been transferred here a month ago from Mabel Bassett Correctional Center as part of my transition into the outside world. My fast-approaching departure was good news, but also scary. Prison hadn't exactly been a five-star hotel—heck, hadn't been a cheap motel, for that matter—but at least I'd had a roof over my head and steady meals. What would I have once I was released? A street corner where I could hold up a will-work-for-food sign? A grocery cart crammed with everything I owned?

The prisoner re-entry program at Transformation Place offered some good deals for ex-cons. But just as I'd suspected, those deals came with catches—policies and procedures.

When I'd stalled as long as I could, I looked up. "This looks ... real interesting. When do you need it back?"

"You should submit your application sixty days before your release. That gives you"—Regina checked her day planner —"about two weeks. By June seventh, at the latest."

I hadn't been too sold on Transformation Place from the beginning. After this meeting, I had more doubts than ever, but my aunt Shannon's place was my only other choice. That came with catches, too.

I told Regina I'd "pray on it"—words I heard church people

say a lot—and gave her the smile I'd used over the years to con store clerks, foster parents, caseworkers, prison guards …. Sometimes it worked. Sometimes it didn't.

"Mm-hmm. Well, take the application and read through it carefully." Regina gathered up her purse and planner. "Send it in if you're interested." Her rush to leave told me this time my smile hadn't worked.

I left the visiting room and headed back to my quad—a section of the building that consisted of five cells with a shared space called a day room. I breathed in the ever-present odor of pine cleaner mixed with a whiff of stale tobacco, a clue that not all the inmates followed the No Smoking rule. I ignored the nameless, faceless women I passed in the beige hallway.

A new girl walked toward me. She was at least a foot shorter than me and was carrying her matrix—prison-issued bedroll, linens, and clothes—in freckled arms no bigger round than twigs. Her thin face, also freckled and surrounded by frizzy, red curlicues, poked above the pile of supplies and made me think of the cherry on top of a sundae. I tried to hold in my laugh, but a chuckle slipped out.

Cherry girl must've mistaken that chuckle for a sign I wanted to be friends. She smiled at me as she passed—a tight, nervous smile. Then she stumbled, probably because her gillies—those ugly canvas prison shoes they made us wear—were at least two sizes too big. Her supplies tumbled to the floor. She got down on all fours, and her pale, pink-tipped fingers snatched at sheets and towels.

All my instincts told me to keep on walking. Prisoners don't have friends. We have people who can be useful to us. No way on earth could this scrawny excuse of a girl ever be useful to me. I wasn't sure why at the time, but I ignored my internal warning and bent over and began snatching up dingy-gray socks and underwear. Without saying anything, I dropped them onto the bedroll she'd re-folded. Before she could even think about talking to me, I walked away.

In my cell, I dialed the combination to my footlocker and tossed in the application.

~

That night in the chow hall, Selena, one of my cellmates, plopped down next to me. Nothing made Selena happier than spreading the latest news, and right now I was the only person around not already yapping with someone else.

She scooted in close and spoke low, like she was some sort of spy. "Hey, chica, you hear about the new girl?"

"Which new girl?"

"Skinny little redhead. Looks like a strong wind would blow her over." Selena's eyes darted around the hall like she was looking for—I don't know—an undercover cop? She shoveled a forkful of lumpy mashed potatoes into her mouth and swallowed. "Stuff going around about her. Scary stuff."

Like I said, Selena loved passing along information. Whether or not it was true didn't matter. I kept quiet and gave her time. In less than five seconds, the dam broke.

"She's loco. Some of the girls in her quad say she was resting on her bunk today and they hear this strange noise. At first they think a mosquito is buzzing around." A high-pitched whine came from Selena's throat, and she wound her index finger through the air like an insect. "Finally, they figure out it's Hallie—that's her name—and she's singing real quiet like. You know what she's singing? *Hymns.*" Selena crossed her arms over her chest and ducked her chin as if she'd just given proof Hallie was one voice-in-her-head away from being an axe murderer.

I opened my eyes big and gave a fake *woo-oo.* Then I gave her my bored look. "That's weird," I said, "but it ain't scary."

"Yeah, well, there's more. Word is she murdered her boyfriend."

I almost snorted my red Jell-O across the table. "That's nuts. You think a murderer is going to be at a minimum-security center?"

Selena tore off a piece of white bread and dipped it in her gravy. "Didn't say she'd been *convicted* of murder. Come on, Gracene. You know people get by with all sorts of crimes. Especially skinny little white girls with hotshot lawyers."

I hated to encourage Selena, but curiosity got the best of me. "So how'd she kill him?"

"Don't know for sure." Selena chewed her food real slow and swallowed. "But I'll find out."

~

Even in mid-May the Oklahoma heat was intense. On Thursday afternoon, I returned from work, took a shower, and went to my cell. I helped with grounds maintenance at the state capital and the governor's mansion. For that I earned just enough money to keep my work from being slave labor. But I liked the assignment. When I was at my job, I could enjoy the outdoors and fresh air and forget about the hours I spent penned up like an animal.

I stretched out on my bunk to grab a quick nap before dinner. That's when I caught sight of my bare feet poking up from the mattress. *Feet? More like skis.* Plain as day I could hear my mama talking: "The minute I first laid eyes on my baby girl, I knew the only name to suit her was some form of Grace."

The minute I learned how to use a dictionary, I looked up the definition of *grace*. It "suited" me like a tutu suits a giraffe or like ballet slippers suit size ten clodhoppers.

I wasn't sleepy anymore, so I got up and opened the footlocker that held the few personal items the state let me keep. Underneath the application, the colored pencils I used for makeup, my raggedy dictionary, and my word journal, I found the photo and pulled it out. I went outside and sat cross-legged under a tree to study it. In the picture, I snuggled on Mama's lap with my arm around her neck, while her arms were around my waist. Both of us smiled wide for the camera. Someone—probably Aunt Shannon—had taken it on my sixth birthday, three days before Mama just up and left. The picture reminded me of what I'd inherited from my mother: goldish-brown eyes, olive skin, brunette hair. It also reminded me of what I hadn't inherited: Mama's tiny body and the gold ring with a ruby stone she always wore. She'd promised to give it to me one day.

I traced Mama's face with my index finger and searched for a hint of fear or sadness behind the smile. Like always, my question came out in a whisper. "Why'd you leave, Mama?"

When I was little, Aunt Shannon convinced me Mama left because she was disgusted with me. "Who'd want a big ol' clumsy girl like you, Gracene?" she'd ask. "No wonder Shirley ran off." When I got older, I figured out no woman would leave her whole life behind just because she was disappointed in her daughter. I knew I wasn't the reason Mama left. I also knew I wasn't reason enough for her to stay. I hated her for that.

My body started heating up, telling me I was about to explode into one of my famous rages. And then I remembered to breathe. In. Out. In. Out. Slow and deep, the way they'd showed me in anger management.

"Gracene, that you doin' a big, bad wolf imitation?"

I tucked the photo under my shirt.

Selena walked up and lowered herself on the ground beside me with an *umph*. "You going to church tonight?"

Resurrection Church had a prison ministry that offered anger management classes and Thursday night services. I'd been attending them for the past three months.

"Do I have a choice?"

"Guess not. Not if you're serious about going to that church place when you get out." She stared at the ground and tore at blades of grass. "*Are* you serious about that? Why would you want to get mixed up with a bunch of boring do-gooders?"

"Well, for starters they offer a rent-free apartment. And they help with finding a job and providing transportation and handling finances. Stuff I'll need until I can get on my feet."

She looked over at me and raised a carefully arched eyebrow. "So you *are* serious."

"Prob'ly not, but until I know for sure, I'm keeping up appearances." I stretched out my legs and leaned against the tree. "Besides, I think those classes are helping. Teaching me things like counting to ten and deep breathing."

"Yeah, right," Selena said. "Chica, the day you learn to control that temper of yours is the day I'll believe in a virgin birth. Might even go back to church myself."

Her chuckling cut off quick when I didn't join in. She pouted for a few seconds and then snapped her fingers. "Oh yeah, speaking of church, I learned some more about the murderer in our mist."

"*Midst*, Selena. Murderer in our *midst*."

"Whatever," she grumbled. "Gracene, you and that dictionary you always carry around can be real pains. And it's weird the way you write down words in that little notebook of yours."

I didn't say anything. In a few seconds, Selena's eagerness to share more gossip trumped her disgust with my dictionary habit. She scooted in close. "Anyway, *mist* or *midst*, you're never going to believe this. Guess how little carrot-top murdered her boyfriend?" She shifted her eyes sideways at me. "She 'baptized' him. To death."

Her smug expression faded under my blank gaze.

"You're right," I said. "I don't believe it." I picked up a small dirt clod and chunked it as far as I could. "It's pure crap."

"No, listen. It makes sense." She lowered her voice. "Seems Hallie and her boyfriend robbed a gas station and were making their getaway in a stolen car. She was driving and must've lost control on a bridge. The car plowed through the guardrail and landed in the creek below." Selena's eyes grew wide. "When the police caught up with them, Hallie was screaming and crying and holding her boyfriend's head under the water."

"Selena," I said, "I've seen this girl, okay? She can't weigh no more than ninety pounds soaking wet. How on earth could she hold someone under water long enough to drown him? Wasn't the boyfriend fighting or struggling?"

She was quiet for a minute and scrunched her forehead like she was thinking hard. "Don't know," she said like she hated to admit it. "Some of the details are a little fuzzy."

Seemed to me there was a lot that was "a little fuzzy" about this story. I was disgusted I'd wasted my time listening to it.

"Gotta go." I stood and brushed dirt and grass from the seat of my pants. "Need to eat something before the bus for church comes."

In the chow hall, me and Selena grabbed our food and sat at our usual table. I'd just filled my mouth with beans when Selena nudged me in the ribs.

"There she is!" She half-whispered, half-shouted, like she'd spotted a celebrity. Or a terrorist.

I followed her line of sight and saw Hallie carrying a food tray. Something was different. She didn't look as helpless as the first time I saw her. She sat at a table and gave the women there a wide smile. They ignored her. Then she folded her hands under her chin, closed her eyes, and started praying. *Out loud.* I knew this because I could see her lips moving and because the other women were gaping as if her head had done a three-sixty spin. But nobody said a word.

I'd never seen such a performance. Yeah, there were women in prison who went to church and prayed, but they never put on this kind of show.

Selena kept her eyes fastened on Hallie. "See, I told you." She circled the side her head with her finger. "Loco."

I didn't necessarily agree. Hallie could be crazy, or she could be crazy smart.

When I was five years old, my cousins Cindy and Beth Ann wouldn't let me ride their bikes.

"Go away, Jumbo," Cindy snarled at me one day. "If you sit on my bike, you'll break it."

I ran to Mama crying. She drew me onto her lap and pressed my head to her chest. "Pay no attention to those runts, Gracene. They're just jealous because you're so pretty and they're little pinch-faced rats." She smoothed my hair from my face. "One day you'll find out that being strong and healthy is a blessing."

I doubt Mama had prison in mind when she gave me that advice, but she'd been right on the money. Prison ran a close second to purgatory on my list of worst places to hang out, but at least my size kept people from hassling me. I'm sure that wasn't the case with Hallie. For someone as tiny—and as weird—as her, prison could be the tenth circle of hell. Maybe she'd figured out the best way to survive it.

CHAPTER TWO

prevenient—*coming before; antecedent*
void—*without contents; empty*

I SAT WITH FIFTEEN OTHER WOMEN AT SOME RICKETY FOLDING tables in a musty classroom. Our ages ranged from twenty-something to fifty-something, and we came in assorted shapes and shades.

Kenneth, pastor of Resurrection Church and the class leader, passed around handouts. "Ladies, tonight we're going to talk about managing our anger by letting go of the past."

The talking died down. Some of the women studied the pages. Others didn't even bother to pick them up. I was one of those.

I leaned back in my chair and crossed my arms over my chest. I'd been going to counseling sessions since I was thirteen. Letting go of the past was always a favorite topic. I could've taught this class myself, but instead of volunteering, I stretched my legs under the table and zoned out.

Right before I dozed off, I remember Kenneth saying, "I'm not saying actions don't carry consequences ..." Yawn. I'd heard it all before.

Forty minutes later, someone nudged me, and I woke up and stood for the closing prayer.

~

We had a fifteen minute break before the church service began, so I went outside to grab a smoke. Alisha, one of the girls in my class, sat beside me on a bench, and we both lit a roll-up—skinny cigarettes we'd rolled ourselves.

A guy who looked to be in his late thirties, maybe early forties, walked by. I'd seen him a couple of times before, and he caught my attention because he looked so out of place. The first time I saw him, I thought he might be a narc, but that couldn't be because he didn't even try to blend in. His short, brown hair was combed with an arrow-straight side part, and he always wore crisp jeans and a knit shirt with a collar. Unlike most of this Thursday night crowd, there wasn't a tattoo or piercing on him anywhere—at least, not one I could see.

That night, he glanced over at Alisha and me and gave us a quick nod. Then he ducked his chin and hurried on by. That was another thing about him. He was kind of a snob—always too busy to wave or even smile. Alisha returned the nod, but I didn't bother.

"Good lesson tonight." Alisha flicked her cigarette ashes onto the ground. "You know, what Kenneth said about people holding on to the past and all."

I wasn't in the mood for a heart-to-heart, so I finished my cigarette, not saying a word, and stood up. "Music's starting. Gotta go." I strolled inside the sanctuary, leaving her to finish her smoke.

I claimed a pew near the back and sat next to a girl I didn't know. While the praise band—guitar, keyboard, and drums—tuned up, I watched people shuffle in. Lots of laughing and hugging was going on. When the band cranked out a praise song, everyone stood and clapped or waved their hands in the air. In case someone was watching, I joined in.

We got through the announcements, the offering, and a few more songs, and then Kenneth got up to preach. I slumped in my seat and studied the inside of the building. The arched beams and stained-glass windows were pretty, but the scratched pews and stained carpet seemed better fits for this crowd—people who also showed signs of heavy wear.

"Have you ever felt like you have a hole in your heart?" I heard Kenneth ask. I looked toward the front of the church, where he was tapping his fist against his chest.

That question brought my plans for a second nap to a halt. When Mama deserted me, she'd left a huge, gaping space—a void —right in that very place.

"It's a God-shaped hole," he said. "And nothing or no one can fill it except God. Some church people have a term for it: preve-nient grace—the grace that comes before. That's just a fancy way of saying even before you know or acknowledge him, God is reaching out to you. He wants a relationship with you. He wants to fill that space."

Kenneth went on to say more, but I didn't hear it. My mind was stuck on the idea of prevenient grace. Like a lot of church stuff, it didn't make sense to me. But there was one thing I knew for certain: That kind of grace didn't apply to me any more than the kind that meant *charm* or *beauty*.

When Mama walked out on me, she changed my life forever— and not in a good way. She left me to grow up on my own— without someone who'd always be in my corner, who'd always have my back. When someone called me "ugly" or "clumsy," no one was there to assure me I wasn't. When things happened that I didn't understand—like growing boobs or having periods—no one was there to explain them. Mama had left me to fight life's battles all by myself, both as a kid and as a young woman. And then there was the monster battle I was still fighting—and losing. Every. Single. Day.

No, the hole in my heart wasn't God-shaped. It was Mama-shaped. And I'd filled it with hate and anger … and guilt.

Kenneth brought his sermon to a close, and we stood for the final song. This time it was a slow, sad one. Everyone was singing soft, with their heads bowed, when a thin, twangy voice drowned out the others. I raised my eyes and saw people grinning and nudging each other and looking toward the front of the church. I looked, too, and saw two bony, milk-white hands, lifted high in the air.

The girl next to me leaned over. "Who's doing all that howling?" she whispered.

"That's Hallie," I said. "*Howl-ey* Roller Hallie."

We both snickered.

~

The usual sounds of clattering dishes and mumbling women filled the chow hall. I was sitting at a table with Selena and three other girls from our quad, but we weren't talking much—not even Selena. Out of the blue, she poked me with her elbow.

"Ouch!" I yelled. "What the—"

"Shhh! Don't look up." Selena kept her eyes on her food. "She's coming this way."

"Who? What're you—"

"Good evening, ladies. May I join you?" Hallie stood at the end of our table and talked like she was joining us for tea.

Prisoners have certain unspoken rules. One of those is a person doesn't walk up to a table and request permission to sit down. But I didn't say anything. Instead I shrugged and scooted down to make room—*lots* of room—on the end of the bench.

Hallie took a seat and placed her paper napkin in her lap. Then she turned to me. "We haven't been formally introduced.

You're Gracene, right? I'm Hallie." She smiled, this time a wide, open-lipped smile that showed a mouthful of tiny little teeth. "I saw you at church last night. Would you like to join me in giving thanks?" She held out her hand to me with the palm up.

Everyone at our table froze, me included. I couldn't swallow, let alone answer her.

I heard a gurgle coming from Selena's throat like she was choking. Then she slapped her hand over her mouth, and her whole body began to shake.

She elbowed me again. "Go ahead, Gracene. Say a prayer with *Howl*-ey Roller Hallie." Everyone at the table—except for me and Hallie—exploded in laughter.

"Where'd you hear that?" I asked Selena.

"Some woman at work today. Everybody's saying it. C'mon, Gracene, admit it. It's funny."

The name wasn't nearly as funny as it had been last night. I shrugged. "I guess."

Selena's pouty mouth showed she'd expected a bigger reaction. "Well, you at least gotta admit it fits."

I glanced over at Hallie, who'd taken her prayer into extra innings. I was about to agree that "Yeah, the name fit," when I noticed the red splotches on her neck and a tiny wet spot at the corner of her eye.

Suddenly I was in middle school, walking through the crowded lunch room with my tray of food. A boy's voice shouted, "Look out! It's Godzilla!" and chants of "Godzilla Gracene!" followed. All around me, fingers were pointing, and jeering faces yelled out the hated nickname I'd been given the first day of sixth grade. Heat spread from the bottom of my feet to the top of my head. Just when I thought I'd burst into flames, I hurled that tray.

The crash of dishes and silverware hitting a concrete wall brought me back to the chow hall, which had grown deathly quiet. Before the shockwaves lifted and the catcalls began, I stomped out.

I went to my cell and plopped down on my bunk. At six o'clock I reported for head count in the day room. Most evenings after head count, I hung around in there and watched a couple of TV shows, but that night I slunk back to my cell. I didn't want to answer any questions about the flying tray in the chow hall. In my bunk I was pouting about the unfairness of growing up practically an orphan, of being a big freak, of never catching a break, when a visitor crashed my pity party.

"Gracene, we need to talk." Lou, the case manager for our quad, was standing just inside the open doorway of my cell.

I'd been expecting this visit. "Here or your office?"

"No one's around. Here will do." She leaned against the concrete blocks of the cell wall and crossed one ankle over the other. "So what's this I'm hearing about a melt-down in the dining hall?"

I'm not one to volunteer a lot of personal information, but I knew Lou could be trusted. I told her about the nickname I'd given Hallie and how mad it had made me to hear it repeated.

"Hallie didn't throw her tray," Lou said. "Seems to me this might be more about you than her."

Although I didn't want to, I went on to tell Lou about Godzilla Gracene. "I felt bad about making up a mean nickname for Hallie," I said. "But you know how prison is. If someone sees any little weakness at all in you, they pounce. I couldn't apologize to Hallie, and I couldn't stick up for her. Throwing that tray seemed to be the best way to end the whole matter."

Lou tapped her index finger against her lips. "Well, Gracene, here's the deal. You're one of the few women in the system who's managed to stretch a four-year sentence into six. As far as I know, there aren't any geriatric wings in a prison, but you're going to need one if you get into any more fights." She paused and stared at the floor. "Look, you worked hard to make it to this facility. I know you've been attending your anger-management

15

classes regularly, and I've seen big improvement in your temper. So here's what I'm going to do."

She let me off with a warning that one more incident like tonight and she'd write me up and fine me.

I had to keep my temper in check for the next few weeks. I figured the best way to stay out of trouble was to avoid people, something I was pretty good at. After Saturday morning breakfast, I took my dictionary and journal outside and sat at a picnic table. I was looking up the word *prevenient* when a shadow came between me and the page.

"May I join you?"

The squeaky voice caused my neck muscles to tighten. I kept my head down and went into my breathing routine. "I don't own the table."

Only in Hallie's world would that have sounded like an invitation. She slid onto the bench across from me and talked nonstop to the top of my head.

∼

I don't know where Hallie got the idea we were tight. She started following me around like some stray kitten I'd made the mistake of feeding. I was working hard to stick to my plan of avoiding people, but no matter where I was—the chow hall, the day room, outdoors—Hallie found me.

I usually ignored her, but on Tuesday evening, after a particularly frustrating day, I fired on her with both barrels. I was stretched out on my bunk, studying my dictionary, when, in her annoying, mousy way, she appeared at the open door to my cell.

"Would you like some company?" she asked.

I slapped the dictionary onto the mattress. "Can't think of anything I want less. And because you seem to be too thick-skulled to take a hint, let me make this real clear. I don't need a friend, I don't want a friend. And if I ever do, it sure as hell won't be you."

Her eyes grew shiny with tears, and red blotches rose up her neck to her cheeks. "I can see this isn't a good time for you," she said with a trembly smile. "I'll check with you later."

I watched her walk away with her head held high. I had to hand it to that girl. Nothing discouraged her. *Nothing.*

After a week of being stalked by her, my patience was worn thin as tissue paper. I'd done so much deep breathing lately I thought any minute I might pass out. On Friday night I was holed up in my cell again, trying to chill. I sat on my bunk with my colored pencils and experimented with new ways to do my eyes. It didn't take long for that to grow old, so I went back to my foot-locker to get my dictionary and journal. I dug to the bottom of the locker and uncovered the application to Transformation Place that was due in about a week. Going there still didn't interest me, but I figured it couldn't hurt to thumb through it.

In my bunk, I flipped through the pages—*thirty-eight* of them. It looked like a lot of work for something that would probably never happen, but there wasn't anything better to do. I leaned against my pillow and read.

The application asked all kinds of irritating questions about my life. I didn't consider most of that information any of their business. But the instructions were clear: *You must fill out the entire application.* To make matters worse, the first two words warned *Be HONEST.* Crraaap.

I skipped all the feel-good stuff like the "Thank you for your interest" and the Mission Statement and went straight to the hard part—the requirements. I was relieved when I read *you must have a desire to change.* Yep, I could meet that one, alright. I wanted everything about my entire life to change. I kept reading.

The *dos* and *don'ts* weren't tough; they were impossible. I would be expected to find a full-time job, pay my own utility bills, and make restitution to the state. All that *and* start a savings account. Also, I'd attend several required meetings a week and help out with chores around the apartment complex. There were lots of *no*'s: no alcohol or drugs, no unapproved visitors, no loud partying, no cussing, no sex on the premises, no firearms, no porn, no illegal activity. The list pretty much banned my entire pre-prison life.

I was ready to toss the application again, this time into the trash. Why fill it out? I could never in a million years follow all those rules.

I got up from my bunk, but instead of going to the trash can, I returned to my locker and pitched the application back in. Something told me it might still come in useful.

The next few weeks passed slower than the time between parole hearings. The only interesting part of my life was figuring out ways to dodge Hallie. One Sunday afternoon I was in my bunk avoiding her, when word came I had a guest. I walked into the visiting room and didn't recognize the skinny, hunched-over figure from the back. I barely recognized her when she turned around.

CHAPTER THREE

ambience—*mood, quality, atmosphere of an environment or milieu*
sinister—*threatening or portending evil, harm, or trouble; ominous*

"AUNT SHANNON."

Me and Aunt Shannon hadn't seen or talked to each other since before I went to prison. Right after coming to Kate Barnard's, I'd sent word I needed to talk to her. When I didn't hear back, I figured she'd written me off. Again. Now we sat on opposite sides of a table and sized up each other.

"Don't look like prison's been too hard on you, Gracene," Aunt Shannon said between wheezes. "You look strong and healthy as ever."

This wasn't a compliment. She'd ridden me all my life about my size. Never let me forget I was bigger than all the other females in the family.

In the past, I would've come back with some smart-mouthed remark, like, "Too bad I can't say the same about you." But my situation had changed. For now I needed to stay on her good side. So I counted in my head.

I couldn't believe how much Aunt Shannon had aged in six

years. She looked more like eighty than fifty. As a kid, I'd always thought of her as just being mean, but I guess she'd also been attractive in a grungy sort of way. Men were constantly sniffing around her—men who must've liked her slender figure and too-tight clothes; men who didn't care that her fried blonde hair had black roots or that she smelled like an ashtray. Of course, they also might've hung around because she was a pushover for anything in pants, even worthless freeloaders.

Today she looked like a bag of bones with a face that had worn out three bodies. She opened her mouth to say something but broke into a phlegmy cough that almost made me gag.

"You seen a doctor about that?" I asked. Her health didn't really concern me. I just couldn't think of anything else to say.

She continued her hacking while she waved off my question with the back of her hand. "Just a smoker's cough," she said when she could finally talk. She took a tissue out of her pocket and wiped her eyes and around her mouth. "I hear you're getting out soon."

"Two weeks."

"Any plans?"

"A few ideas. Nothing for certain right now." I shrugged. "Something'll come up." I hoped my answer made me sound a lot more confident than I felt.

Aunt Shannon nodded and didn't look at me. I could tell she didn't want to offer me a place to stay, and Lord knows I didn't want to ask. I picked at a cuticle while she drummed her fingers on the table. Neither of us spoke.

"I have one idea in mind," I said at last. "A place where I can stay 'til I get a job and get my feet on the ground." I saw her whole body relax.

"That'd be good," she said. "You know Beth Ann and Cindy have moved back home with six kids between 'em. Floyd's working somewhere in Montana, but Bobby and Cody never left, so my place is busting at the seams right now."

I could picture it. From her first divorce settlement, Aunt Shannon had ended up with a few acres and a ramshackle house. All the time I lived there it had been crammed with Aunt Shannon's five kids by three different daddies and an endless parade of male deadbeats and sometimes their kids. Four cats had free rein of the house, and no one ever cleaned up after themselves or the cats. The place had all the ambience of a bus station.

"And, oh yeah, Del's back." Aunt Shannon threw in this last bit of information like it had just come to her. Like it was no big deal.

But it was a big deal—a *huge* deal. Almost twenty-two years had passed since I'd last seen him, but the mention of Del's name still made me break out in goose bumps.

I remembered him as smelly and dirty and the worst kind of evil. Sometimes his pale green eyes would light up with mischief, coaxing us kids to pull some crazy stunt like putting rocks in Aunt Shannon's hubcaps. We knew we'd catch all kinds of hell when we were caught, but the fun would be worth it. Other times his eyes would narrow into slits, and his face would grow dark as a thunderhead. At those times, me and my cousins couldn't get away from him fast enough. Even kids could tell bad things—sinister things—were going on behind those creepy eyes.

"So he's back." I couldn't keep my voice from shaking. "Been a long time. He just show up out of the blue?"

Aunt Shannon nodded. "You could say that. After him and Shirley took off, I didn't hear from him at all. Every so often I'd get wind of some gossip ... he was growing pot out in California ... running rides for a traveling carnival. A few years ago, I heard he was serving time for cooking dope somewhere around Poteau." After another coughing fit, Aunt Shannon placed her elbows on the table and leaned on them like she didn't have the strength to sit up straight. "Then a few weeks ago he shows up, no explanation, no nothing. Acting like he hadn't been gone for over twenty years … like he'd just run to the store for a case of beer or some cigarettes."

My face started heating up. "Did he say anything about Mama?"

She gave her head a quick shake. "Nope."

"Did you even ask him about her?"

"Oh, for pity's sake, Gracene. I asked, okay? He said Shirley and him parted ways shortly after they ran off together. Says he hasn't seen or heard from her since."

Aunt Shannon had always claimed Del and Mama ran off together because they disappeared on the same night, but I never believed it. Mama hated Del. They locked horns like two stags in mating season, only they fought year 'round. Still, I thought he might've heard something.

Aunt Shannon pinched the bridge of her nose and spoke in a tired, thin voice. "You're a grown-up woman, Gracene. Time to face facts. Your mama ain't coming back. *Ever.* There's nothing here she'd want to come back for."

I'd heard stuff like this the whole time I was growing up. Today—just like always—it left me gutted. But instead of slouching and hugging my middle, I sat up straighter. Years of practice had taught me to bluff my way through pain.

Aunt Shannon regained enough of her energy to go on. "Del made parole a few weeks ago and didn't have nowhere to stay, so I let him crash at my place for a while. Guess I always did have a soft spot in my heart for ol' Del." Her laugh came out in a snort. "Even if he was an SOB."

She had a soft spot, alright—for ol' Del and about a dozen other losers—but it was in her head, not her heart. She collected boyfriends like she collected the wind chimes that hung all around her property. And like those chimes that weren't good for anything but making constant racket in the Oklahoma wind, her choice of boyfriends never made sense, either. I once heard her threaten to blow off Del's nether regions if he ever set foot on her property again. And here she was, twenty-two years later, welcoming him with open arms. I guess with her looks gone, she was growing desperate for whatever she could get.

"Well, it'd be crowded," she said in a whiny voice, "but you're family. I guess we could always squeeze in one more if we had to." Her invitation was as warm as a county sheriff's request to visit his jail. She pushed against the table top and stood. "Let me know what you decide."

I watched her shuffle toward the door on her skinny legs. *Family.* Aunt Shannon had never treated me like family after Mama left. She'd made this offer only because she knew I'd been scared to death of Del when I was little. She figured if he was there, no way would I move back into that house. But two things she hadn't figured on: I was a lot bigger now and didn't scare as easy as I used to ... and I was also desperate for whatever I could get.

～

Around one in the morning, the nightmare that used to visit me on a regular basis stopped by again. The one where a child stands with her nose pressed against a rusty screen and stares into a moonless, starless sky. The dark hides everything, but she knows what's beyond the window: a rickety shed draped with cobwebs, a scum-covered pond surrounded by a tangle of woods. Hot, muggy air pushes through the screen and settles on the child's goose-fleshed skin. She shudders and scrambles back to the bed she shares with two bigger girls. Chirps and croaks and far-off coyote yelps mingle with her bedmates' deep, steady breathing. Suddenly the tinkling of a wind chime drowns out all sounds except that of a man's raspy voice filtering through the window. "Heeeey, little girl, I know you're in there. Come out and play with me." She pulls the bed sheet over her head and curls into a ball as the man's low, mean laugh is replaced by angry shouts. And then the shouts are replaced by screams.

I jerked awake, soaked in sweat and shivering. My heart was pounding against my ribs like it was trapped in my chest and trying to break out. I listened to the sounds of women moaning and crying out in their sleep while I waited for my heartbeat to calm down. I didn't recognize the little girl or the voice in that dream. And, like always, I woke up before discovering whether the same person was doing the laughing and the screaming or who it was. But I did recognize the shed and the pond. They were on Aunt Shannon's place.

A soft light glowed from an EXIT sign that stayed on 'round the clock. I usually cussed that light because it kept me awake. That night I was grateful for it. I went to my footlocker and dug through it for a cigarette. When I couldn't find one, I slammed the lid down.

Selena's sleepy voice came from the bunk above me. "What the hell, Gracene? Do you know what time it is?"

I climbed back into bed, wide awake. I didn't need a shrink to interpret that nightmare. Returning to Aunt Shannon's was more than a bad idea. It was a dangerous one.

I thought about that lesson at church—the one that claimed people wanted to cling to their pasts, no matter how horrible. It was a big, fat lie. I would've volunteered for brain surgery if it could cut out all my bad memories. But since surgery wasn't available, I had to come up with another plan. I returned to my locker and took out a pencil and the application to Transformation Place.

This time, by the light of the EXIT sign, I read the parts I'd skipped before. I read the Vision Statement Regina had pointed out—the one about change being possible. I didn't believe it for a minute, but I started writing anyway.

Education: dropped out in 10th grade; grades were mostly Cs and Ds; completed GED at Mabel Bassett Correctional Center.

Alcohol/chemical use? experimented with marijuana; heavy drinking during one period of my life; underwent required substance abuse treatment at Mabel Bassett; have been drug- and alcohol-free for over seven years.

How much do you owe in court costs, fines, etc.? $10,000

Describe your legal history by completing the chart below. I filled in the chart with a string of convictions that began when I was eighteen. My crimes had fancy legal names, but basically, all of them had to do with check-forging and DUIs.

I felt only a mild twinge of guilt as I wrote. I guessed I was sorry for the trouble I'd caused some people, but as far as I was concerned my "debt to society" had been paid with six years of my life. And I would still be paying on it for a long time after my release. But as I read over my list of crimes, a shocking fact jumped out at me. My worst offense—the one I could never undo or make restitution or ask forgiveness for, the one that still tormented me every waking minute—wasn't even on the list.

Filling out the legal information had disturbed me, but at least there'd been plenty of information to write down. That wasn't the case when it came to *Family History*: Never knew my dad; mother deserted me when I was six; was raised by a hateful aunt until I entered the state foster care system at age thirteen.

I thought I'd answered all the hard stuff. Then I came to the *Spiritual* section and read the question: *What does "Higher Power" mean to you?*

By the time my prison sentence was handed down, I'd already sworn off alcohol. I was never rocket scientist material, but I was plenty smart enough to figure out drinking led to poor decisions. And one of those poor decisions had led to the worst one of my life. But DUIs were on my record, so I was required to take part in a drug treatment program at Mabel's.

I thought about that program as I struggled to fill in this section of the application. It had instructed participants to turn over addiction problems to "a Power greater than ourselves, or

God as we understood him." My understanding wasn't much. Wasn't much as in *hardly at all*. And what little I did understand made me angry more than trusting. If God was all-powerful and loving, why would he allow so much suffering? Why would he let little children get cancer? Be abused? Be deserted—or worse—by their own mothers?

But Transformation Place was a church program, set up by and for Christians. I couldn't write on the application that I sort of believed in the existence of a higher power but wasn't too sold on how loving it was. I chewed on my pencil and my fingernails and racked my brain for something to say that would make me sound at least halfway religious. At one point, I was ready to chuck the whole idea. I flung the pencil and application across my cell. Then I remembered my only other choice—living with Aunt Shannon—and went and got them.

I stared at that *Higher Power* question for over an hour before it came to me that I'd been pulling con jobs since I was eight and gotten away with most of them. If I could convince Aunt Shannon I didn't take twenty bucks out of her purse or could talk a prison guard into lending me a cell phone, surely I could persuade a bunch of do-gooders I'd found religion.

Ideas began to flow like beer from a keg. The tap clogged when the warning *Be HONEST* flashed through my mind. For a split-second I reconsidered what I was doing. Then I thought, screw that. I've been ignoring warnings all my life. No reason to stop now.

The ideas flowed again, and I finished that application right before sun-up.

CHAPTER FOUR

pessimism—*the tendency to see or anticipate only bad or undesirable outcomes*
inquiry—*an act of seeking information by questioning; interrogation*
fable—*a short tale used to teach a moral lesson*

ON THE LAST DAY OF JULY, I STEPPED OUTSIDE THE CHAIN-LINK fence and into the parking lot of Kate Barnard's. I had the clothes on my back—jeans and a T-shirt—and a paper sack. The sack held my dictionary and journal, my colored pencils, the picture of me and Mama, seven pairs of clean underwear, three bras, and fifteen dollars.

Right before my release that morning, Selena had given me her brother's address. "If things don't work out with that church program," she said, "Marco can find you a place to crash and maybe set you up in his business."

I thanked her and stuffed the number into my pocket, although I didn't plan on using it. Marco's "business" was a large part of the reason Selena was locked up.

In the parking lot, I looked around and fought back panic

when I didn't see anyone. Then an aging minivan pulled up, and Regina popped out.

"Sorry I'm late. Got hung up at a railroad crossing." She squeezed my shoulders in a side hug. "Congratulations, girl! This is one of the favorite parts of my job." She dug her cell phone out of her purse and held it up. "Smile!" The camera clicked. "Always like to document residents experiencing their first moments of freedom."

I studied the picture she held in front of me. It looked like a mug shot.

"Let's get you home." She climbed back into the van and apologized again for being late. "I always try to be here as soon as a person walks through those gates. Can't imagine a scarier feeling than being released and having no one waiting for you."

"You weren't that late." I didn't want to admit how relieved I'd been when I saw her.

"I'm still marveling over how things worked out," she said on the drive to Transformation Place. "Like I told you, we usually require sixty days to approve an application. But your request came in just as another one got cancelled, so we were able to expedite the process."

"I guess I was—" I caught myself right before saying *lucky* "—blessed." Then I gave Regina my best church-people smile.

Ten minutes later, we pulled into the parking lot of an old apartment complex. "This is it," she said, coming to a stop. She nodded toward the building that looked as hot and tired as I felt. "You ready?"

With the neck of my T-shirt, I wiped at some sweat trickling down my chest. *Am I ready? No time like the present to find out.* I climbed from the van and followed Regina through a squeaking gate in a stone wall.

On the other side of the gate, the U-shaped apartment building surrounded a courtyard. The landscaping—if you could call it that—consisted mostly of sun-baked dirt, cement, and gravel. In its center, some fool with more optimism than green thumb had planted rosebushes that were nothing but scraggly branches with a few moldy leaves. My "home" for the next six months wouldn't win any house or garden awards, but I'd seen worse. A lot worse.

Regina led me past apartments and what looked like hand-me-down patio furniture and garage sale odds and ends. Then we climbed some stairs to the second story and a corner apartment. Regina took a key from her pocket and put it in the lock.

Beneath the eaves of an apartment two doors down, three wind chimes tinkled softly. I slapped my hands over my ears.

Regina looked at me. "You okay? You're white as a sheet."

I lowered my hands and gave my head a toss. "Just wondering why on earth anyone in Oklahoma would want wind chimes," I grumbled.

Regina eyed me for a second and went back to jiggling the key. "I hear ya. On a still day like today, they're not so bad. But when 'the wind comes sweeping,' they're more annoying than the midnight yowl of a tomcat."

Annoying. I was thinking more along the lines of terrifying.

Regina continued to wiggle the key. "Need to get Jake to look at this lock. He's one of our residents—a regular genius when it comes to fixing things. Sure going to miss him when he leaves." She worked a while longer and gave a little shout when the key finally turned. She held the door open and motioned me in. "Folks from a local church worked on this unit for weeks. It's real nice."

I pressed my lips together to hold in the *yeah, right* about to slip out. Whether it had been at Aunt Shannon's, government shelters, or foster homes, I'd been living with other people's cast off junk all my life. I couldn't recall any of it ever being "real nice."

But what I found inside the apartment surprised me. I breathed in the smells of new paint and Windex, as Regina gave a quick tour of the living room that flowed into a connected dining room and kitchen. Then we inspected the bathroom and bedroom. The apartment was fitted out with furniture that matched and was in good condition. There were even pictures on the walls. For the first time in a long time, I let a glimmer of hope poke through the layer of pessimism I wore like a hazmat suit.

"Think this'll do?" Regina asked.

I gave her a cautious smile. "Just like you said. 'Real nice.'"

"Good! You know, we generally have two residents to an apartment. You'll have a roommate before long." She checked her watch and walked to the door. "I'll give you some time to settle in, and then you can meet me in my office in an hour. It's downstairs, just off the community room. We'll go over the policies and procedures together."

My neck and shoulders tensed. That glimmer of hope I'd just experienced faded faster than a shooting star. *Policies and procedures* reminded me that even if Transformation Place didn't charge rent, living here wouldn't be free.

I took another tour of the apartment, starting in the kitchen. Like a nosy guest, I snooped through drawers and cabinets filled with silverware, dishes, detergent—everything needed for setting up housekeeping. The dining area was a little crowded with a table, two chairs, and a hutch, but it looked like a nice place to have meals. In the bathroom I found towels, rags, soap, toothpaste, and a toothbrush. I tested the plumbing by turning on the hot water and then flushing the toilet. Everything seemed to be in working order, so I moved on to the bedroom.

I'd always bragged about being a loner. Early in life I learned the only person I could depend on or trust was me. Even in prison, where I was surrounded by people all day every day, I kept to myself as much as possible. Living alone in this apartment would've suited me just fine. But the twin beds reminded me I'd soon have a roommate.

~

"Come on in, Gracene. You don't have to knock." Regina opened the door and motioned me inside. "This apartment is the community room and my office, not a private residence anymore." She walked into the kitchen, and I heard a fridge door open. "Something to drink? Soda? Water?"

"No, thanks."

She re-appeared with a diet drink in her hand and motioned for me to follow her. In an office behind the community room, she took a seat at a large, built-in desk that faced a wall. Papers were stacked neatly on top. She swiveled her office chair around and faced me. "Have a seat," she said, nodding toward a couple of wingback chairs.

I sat in one of them and pressed down hard on my knees to keep them from bouncing. My life had taught me some good lessons about reading people. I could spot a fraud a mile off. With her serious brown eyes and matter-of-fact way of talking, Regina struck me as the real deal. She also struck me as someone else who could spot a fraud. I'd have to be on my guard around her.

"Relax. I'm your supervisor, not your warden," she said. "I know it takes a while to get used to that." She leaned back in her chair and pulled the tab on the soda can. "Did you find everything you need in your apartment?"

"Yeah. A lot more than I expected."

"Good. How're you fixed for clothes?"

"Right now I'm wearing everything I own except for my extra underwear."

"Mm-hmm." She took a sip from the can and set it on her desk. "That's usually the case. When we finish here, I'll take you shopping."

"I don't have much money," I said.

"Don't worry about that. At our exclusive boutique, the Resurrection Church Clothes Closet, everything has been

31

donated. The clothes are clean and"—she made quotation marks with her fingers—"'gently worn.' You'll like the prices. Everything's free."

She reached over to pick up the papers on her desk and laid them on her lap. After she read out loud that endless list of impossible rules, she looked up. "You okay with all that?"

I nodded.

"Good." She took a few pages from the bottom of the stack. "Just one more thing—a little business to take care of." A crease formed between her eyes as she reviewed those papers. "The bad news is you owe a chunk of change in fees and fines. The good news is you can wait to start repayment until you finish the program here."

I wasn't so sure there was any good news. On my first day of so-called freedom, I was already buried under an avalanche of rules and a mountain of debt.

"Let's see," she said. "You owe fees for court costs in Logan and Oklahoma counties. Also, you owe them for the hospitality they extended you in their county jails." She raised her eyes to look at me. "You understand—right?—that you have to report to them within seventy-two hours to arrange your payments. Otherwise, they'll tack on another fine."

"Man," I grumbled, "you'd think I worked this off in prison."

"Yeah, they get you coming and going, that's for sure. Be thankful you don't owe child support payments on top of this like some of our residents do." She sat up straight and rubbed the back of her neck like she was as stressed over this as I was. "Just try to take it one day at a time."

She handed me some of the papers. "You've already completed the application and signed the agreement, but I want you to look over them again and see if anything has changed."

I flipped through the thirty-plus pages I'd filled out weeks ago. Today I stopped at the question *What does "Higher Power" mean to you?* I read my answer slowly. I needed to remember what I'd written.

"Higher Power" means there is a heavenly Father who loves me and will take care of me if I listen to him and do what he says. I haven't been very good at that in the past, but now I know that not doing that leads to trouble and unhappiness. I'm already reading my Bible every day, and I attend church whenever I can. I also pray every day. I will keep on doing that when I get out of prison because I am most happy when I am in touch with God.

For the second time that day, panic nearly strangled me. I couldn't believe I'd written that bull. And no way would I be able to keep up this act for six months.

"Everything in order?" Regina raised her eyebrows. "Any changes?"

I seriously thought about throwing the papers on the desk and bolting. At that moment, returning to a life of crime looked a lot easier than pulling off this act.

Someone entered the community room from outside, and the tinkling of wind chimes floated through the open door.

My throat tightened, and the papers shook as I handed them back to Regina. "No changes. Everything looks fine."

Regina drove the van toward Resurrection Church while I studied the list of rules she'd given me. Living at Transformation Place required attendance at residents' meetings on Tuesday nights and church services every Sunday. I was also to continue the anger management classes and attend even more services on Thursday evenings. I had to find a full-time job and save three hundred dollars by the time my six months were up.

I heaved a sigh and dropped the papers onto my lap.

"Something wrong?" Regina asked.

I looked down and shook my head. "I just ... I don't ..."

"Yeah, I know," she said. "Right now it looks hard. Maybe impossible. But do you remember what I told you about the recidivism rate for our graduates?"

"Can't remember," I mumbled.

"Three-point-seven percent. That's opposed to thirty percent if a person doesn't receive help. Think about it. Your chances of returning to prison are almost ten times greater if you don't complete our program. I'd say those odds make a few months of hard work worth it."

I kept my head lowered and considered what she'd said. I raised it just as we passed a gas station.

"Holy sh—moly! Look at the price of gas! Things sure change." I took the cell phone I'd been loaned out of my pocket and stared at it. "Especially technology. I don't even know how to use this thing."

"Yup, change happens." Regina kept her eyes on the road as she talked. "Even people change. That's what Transformation Place is all about."

Uh-oh. That sounded like a sermonette might be on the way. I turned and looked out the passenger window, thinking if I pretended I wasn't listening I could head it off. But I should've known copping an attitude wouldn't discourage Regina.

"What you're facing isn't easy," she said. "Every single person who's gone through Transformation Place has a story. Some more tragic than yours. Take it one day at a time, and most importantly, pray. Make up your mind you're going to succeed no matter what. 'Cause I'm telling you, girl, some of those stories do have happy endings." She flashed a wide smile. "You're looking at one."

She had my full attention with those words, and I turned my face toward her. Unfortunately, she pulled into the parking lot of Resurrection Church before I could ask any questions. She parked the van and took a piece of nicotine gum from her purse.

"Been smoking since I was fourteen," she complained. "Trying to quit. Again." She popped the gum into her mouth and opened the van door. "Let's go shopping."

~

I got off the bus in the Uptown section of Oklahoma City and made my way toward Transformation Place, bummed from another rejection. After two weeks of being turned down for minimum wage jobs any teenager could do, I was on the edge of panic. When you're drowning in debt and there's no money coming in, two weeks can be an eternity.

On my walk I passed a few boarded-up storefronts. But I also passed new businesses that were popping up in this area like dandelions in springtime. An expensive antiques store, an art gallery, a couple of new bars, some ritzy restaurants—they all told me Uptown was snatching at new life. Just like me.

The temperature outside was in the mid-nineties, and inside my apartment wasn't a whole lot cooler. Rent might've been free, but the meter was ticking on my utilities. I poured myself a glass of iced tea and collapsed in the recliner. The thought kept coming to me that I'd done okay with my life of crime. At least until I got caught. I'd had a roof over my head and plenty to eat, and I could pretty much come and go as I pleased. Going back to that life might be easier than trying to survive the straight and narrow. And I'd learned a thing or two. The next time I'd be smart enough not to get caught.

A knock at the door interrupted those thoughts.

"Come in," I yelled. I didn't have the energy to get up.

Regina stuck her head inside the door. "Got a minute?"

What now? A visit from Regina usually meant I'd broken some piddling rule like playing my TV too loud or had gotten notice of another fine or court cost. "Sure, come on in."

"Won't be here long." She took a seat on the edge of the couch and held out an official-looking letter. "Got this today."

I opened the envelope, read the notice, and let it drop in my lap.

"Another fee?" Regina asked.

I moaned and let my head collapse against the recliner.

"That's tough. But we'll get it straightened out. Any luck with the job interview?"

"Nope."

"Darn! Well, don't give up. Something'll turn up. It always does." Springs squeaked as Regina shifted farther back on the couch. "You know the Exodus story, don't you?" she asked finally. "The one about Moses leading the Israelites out of Egypt?"

Well, that was random, I thought. I had no idea where this question had come from, but I was too tired to ask, so I just nodded. I knew the story, not from any Bible studying, but from watching *The Ten Commandments* a couple of times. And I remembered bits of a Disney cartoon.

"So you know," she said, "how the Israelites had been out of Egypt for about fifteen minutes before they started complaining, right? They got a little hungry and thirsty, and suddenly their memories failed them. They forgot all about how miserable they'd been in Egypt and wanted to go back. You remember that?"

If I'd ever heard that part of the story, it had slipped my memory. But I nodded again to hurry this inquiry along.

"A lot of folks don't understand that," Regina said. "They don't understand how the Israelites could forget so quickly how terrible life in Egypt had been." She gave a little huff. "But it's no mystery to me at all. I know exactly how those Israelites felt. When we want to move on and it's a lot harder than we thought it would be, our memories tend to be very short … and selective. We forget about the pain and misery of our past lives. And we forget about the pain we caused others."

I sat perfectly still and closed my eyes. I didn't want to send any sign I was listening to her.

"I like to share my personal story with each resident," she said. "But I try to wait for the right moment—when I think they're ready to hear it."

I opened my eyes. I'd been curious about her since the day she told me she was one of the "happy endings" at Transformation Place.

Regina sat silent with her head tilted and her eyes squinted. Not an "I can't see" squint but an "I'm thinking" one. Finally she spoke.

"My dad was a mean son of a gun. When my mother had taken all of the verbal and physical abuse she could stand, she ran off. Without Mom around to bully, Dad started in on my four younger siblings and me. He worked long hours and assigned us lots of chores to do. If things weren't in perfect order when he got home, there were consequences. *Harsh* consequences." She sat still for a moment, then flinched. "I'll never forget that swishing sound his belt made as he pulled it from the loops on his pants.

"As soon as I graduated from high school, I got married just to get away from home. My husband got a construction job and worked hard. Things were going good for us, but you know how it is. You look around and see what everyone else has, and soon you find yourself wanting more. Then there are kids to feed and clothe. And *they* want more."

"You have kids?" I'd never considered that.

"Two."

I could hear the sadness behind that one-word answer. Regina didn't volunteer any information about them, so I didn't ask.

She went on to tell how keeping up with the Joneses turned into a mountain of unpaid bills. The stress of those bills led to her and her husband's heavy drinking. As could be expected, marriage problems developed, and divorce soon followed.

"I was a single mother with two kids to support, and my drinking problem was getting expensive. I started looking for a way to make extra cash, and I found it. I began embezzling funds from the company I worked for. It was good money and easy ... until I got caught. I spent four years behind bars."

Regina wrapped up her story by telling how she found God—or God found her—when she was in prison. Transformation Place helped her rebuild her life when she got out. "It wasn't easy. Just like you, I searched a long time for a job. My kids were angry with me and still are. They blame me for going to prison and abandoning them. I kicked my alcohol addiction through the prison AA program, but the heavy drinking left me with some health problems."

"Geez," I said when she finished. "You always seem to have it so together. I had no idea."

She shook her head. "I'm not telling you this to get sympathy. I praise God every single day for the good things he's done in my life. If it weren't for him, I would've died in my own personal Egypt years ago." She scooted to the edge of the couch and leaned toward me. "I'm telling you so you'll know I've been where you are—in that place where all those one-more-steps just seem to be leading into more desert. But you have to keep putting one foot in front of the other and reminding yourself things *will* get better if you trust God. What those Israelites hadn't noticed on their journey was that God was providing everything they needed day by day. Back in Egypt they'd had water and a little food, but they'd still been slaves."

On her way out the door, she paused. "Hang in there, girl. I have a feeling good things are right around the corner."

I picked up the letter in my lap, read it again, and let it fall to the floor. That story Regina told about the Israelites and the desert was nothing more than a fable—one of those stories that tell people what they're not supposed to do. But I was disgusted and broke and out of work and out of hope. It would take more than a kid's story to keep me here.

In my bedroom, I pulled the address Selena had given me out of my underwear drawer. I told myself anything was better than living here, begging for loser jobs and barely surviving on hand-outs. Knowing that if I ever did get a job, half of my pay would be going to the state. I stuffed my clothes and belongings into a plastic trash bag and crammed eight dollars—all the money I had in the world—into my pocket.

At the front door, I paused for just a second. I knew leaving Transformation Place was a risky move. If things didn't work out with Marco, my only other option was living with Aunt Shannon. But I convinced myself I could handle that. I was bigger and older now and could protect myself. Anyway, it probably wasn't as bad as I remembered. I sucked in a deep breath and opened the door.

My foot had no more cleared the threshold when a hot breeze stirred and the tinkling of wind chimes floated on the air. My skin broke out in goose bumps, and every nerve in my body went on full alert. I did a fast retreat to the bedroom and unpacked the bag.

CHAPTER FIVE

fluke—*an accidental advantage; stroke of good luck*
facilitator—*a person responsible for leading or coordinating the work
of a group, as one who leads a group discussion*

THE BUS CAME TO A STOP WITH A *WHOOSH*, AND I STEPPED OFF. As
if the day wasn't already hot enough, I was still steaming over
wasting a perfectly good bus pass on a crappy interview for a job
I didn't want. The assistant manager of the busy fast food restaurant hadn't looked a day over fourteen. When I handed him the
application I'd spent thirty minutes filling out, he glanced at it for
about five seconds.

"Thanks," he said, giving me an even quicker glance. "If we're
interested, we'll get in touch."

With that, he folded the application in his back pocket and
began scooping french fries into a container.

I walked down 23rd Street toward my apartment. Under the
late-August sun, the pavement burned my feet through the soles
of my shoes, and my fifteen-minute makeup job was sliding
down my face.

Despite my mood and hurry to get out of the heat, I stopped

in the courtyard at Transformation Place to check the rose-bushes. They were looking better since I'd been spraying them for mites and watering them regularly. One was even sprouting tiny buds. I knelt and gently pressed a new leaf between my thumb and forefinger. Suddenly I saw Mama standing next to a kid version of me while I watered seedlings in a tiny vegetable garden. "Plants, animals, humans," Mama said. "Gracene, there are very few things that won't thrive if you give them plenty of sunshine, water, and TLC."

I stood and brushed my hand on the side of my jeans. Strange advice, I thought, from a woman who—

"Hi, Miss Gracene!"

I looked in the direction of the voice. Despite the ache in my heart, I couldn't hold back my smile. "Hey, Reesie!" I waved at the four-year-old, who sat on the seat of a shiny, pink tricycle. Her sweaty curls stuck to the sides of her face. A ring of purple, probably from a Popsicle, circled her mouth. She gave me a huge grin and pedaled toward me.

"Guess what, Miss Gracene." She stopped just short of my toes. "My big brother and sister are coming to visit tomorrow."

"That's awesome, Reesie! I'll bet you're excited."

"I am. Mommy's excited, too." She took off on her trike like a demolition driver.

I watched her ride away and thought about our last residents' meeting. Reesie's mother, Melissa, had shared between sobs how she longed to get her older kids back. Transformation Place was helping to make that happen, but it was a slow and painful process. My eyes began to sting. Why was it, I wondered, that some mothers would walk barefoot over glass to keep their kids, while others deserted them at the first chance to chase after a selfish dream? A cold fist clamped around my heart. And other mothers did worse.

I went back to my rose inspection but couldn't focus on the plant. Too many *if only*s were circling in my mind: *if only* I'd been more careful ... *if only* I'd laid off the booze ... *if only* I'd listened to my gut instead of—

"That you, Gracene? Can we talk a minute?"

The voice jerked me from the dungeon in my mind where all my regrets were stored. Regina was calling from the community room doorway.

I swore softly so she couldn't hear. I should've been grateful for the rescue, but right now all I wanted was a long soak in a tub of cool water, and her request sounded an awful lot like a summons. Residents were expected to help out with chores and maintenance around the building. Regina probably wanted me to vacuum a vacated apartment or tidy up the community room— jobs I hated.

I sat slumped in her office and gulped a cold drink, enjoying the fizzy burn in my throat.

"How'd the interview go?" she asked.

"Don't think I'll be hearing from them. Management didn't seem very felon friendly."

She leaned back in her chair and rested her hands on her stomach. "Well, maybe that's for the best. I might have something that works better for you. At least temporarily."

My antennae went up. Regina was almost as antsy for me to get a job as I was. No telling what she'd lined up.

"I've been noticing those rose bushes are showing signs of new life," she said.

"They'll survive."

She opened a manila folder with my name on the tab. "And I know while you were at Kate's you worked on a grounds crew at the capital and the governor's mansion."

"That's right."

"I met a man who does landscaping," she continued. "Richard Powers. I thought maybe he could use some help, so I contacted him. He was interested. In fact, he seemed pleased at the prospect of hiring someone with experience."

She had my attention. This sounded a lot more promising than working at a fast food chain or a convenience store.

She picked up a notepad she'd scribbled on and studied it. "He said it can be hot, dirty work and involves some heavy lifting. You up for that?"

"I know what that work's like. Heat and a little dirt don't bother me." I studied my large hand, resting on my large thigh. "And might as well put this super-sized body to some good use."

"I don't know so much about that 'super-sized' stuff," she said, "but this job might be a good fit for you." She lifted an eyebrow. "How about it? Want me to arrange an interview?"

"Sure, why not?" I stood to leave.

"Not so fast! I have some more good news for you."

I sat down again and held back a groan. The news about the job had been good, but that was a fluke. My idea of good news and Regina's hardly ever matched. For instance, she'd thought it was good news that Transformation Place had received a furniture donation I could help pick up and deliver to the storage garage. And it had been good news that since I wasn't working, I could help some church volunteers lay wooden flooring in one of the units.

"Kenneth wants you to assist him with the anger management classes on Thursday nights."

I certainly hadn't seen that one coming. "Uh ... why me? I don't have any training or a psychology degree or anything to qualify ..."

"Relax," she said, with a wave of her hand. "He doesn't want you to plan lessons or do counseling or anything like that. Mostly it's organization stuff, like distributing handouts or getting the room ready for class. You'll be fine." Her face beamed like she'd just announced I'd won the lottery.

Like I said, when it came to good news, Regina and I were seldom on the same page.

～

The very next Thursday, I walked around the beat-up tables at Resurrection Church and distributed handouts to the class. That night's lesson: self-affirmation.

Some of these women I already knew; some were first timers. Some came because they would receive rewards for attending—rewards like time knocked off their sentences or a good word to the parole board. I think some came just to relieve the boredom of prison life. And I suspect a few came because, like me in the beginning, they'd grown desperate enough to try anything.

That night, while Kenneth talked, I wondered why he'd picked me, of all people, to help with this class. Yeah, I'd been attending these sessions for a few months and had learned to manage my angry outbursts most of the time. But there were still times when my insides felt like a volcano about to erupt.

Kenneth always said what we needed to hear, whether we liked it or not. And he kept his cool when someone tried to show how tough she was. I liked that about him. He was laid back but at the same time pulled no punches. I guess that's the reason I'd agreed to help.

So there I was, serving in my new role as "facilitator," with no clue what that even meant, when Macy decided she was about to pass out from the heat. At nineteen, she was the youngest in the group, so she felt she had the most to prove. I understood that kind of thinking.

Like some menopausal old lady, Macy fanned her face, then pointed to the ceiling. "There's no air coming from that vent," she said right in the middle of Kenneth's explanation of "affirmation visualization." She added a couple of cuss words for emphasis.

"Macy, you know that kind of language isn't allowed," Kenneth said calmly. "But I agree it's hot in here. Gracene, you take over. I'll get the maintenance man." He stood and left the room.

A couple of colorful words popped into my own head, but I caught myself before I said them out loud. They were followed by a silent prayer: *Please* don't let anything happen while I'm in charge.

I'd attempted a few desperate prayers in my life. This one, like all the others, didn't make it past the ceiling. I'd no more finished it when Macy climbed onto one of the tables. She stretched up to adjust the vent, but it was just out of her reach, so, like an idiot, she started jumping. Every time she landed, that old table rattled and shook like it was about to fall apart.

"Macy, stop it and get down right now!" I could feel my face getting red hot. "And quit showing off. No one's impressed."

Macy stopped jumping. She looked me in the eye, and her mouth curled into a sneer.

I'd had enough challenges in my lifetime to know one when I saw it. And I hadn't met the woman yet who could make me back down—unless she had a gun or a knife. Pretty sure that Macy wasn't armed, I shot out of my chair, knocking it onto the floor. The clang of metal on tile echoed through the room. After a group gasp, all the women grew quiet. I could tell by their wide eyes and open mouths every one of them was expecting—or hoping—for me and Macy to come to blows.

I'd stood with the intention of grabbing Macy's arm and pulling her from the table, but during that span of silence, something stopped me. Something that told me to look at Macy. *Really* look at her.

It's funny how many images can flash across a person's brain in just a few seconds. I was staring at Macy, but what I saw was myself—my younger self. I saw the same cocked head, tucked chin, hands on the hips. I saw a girl convinced she had to take on the world all by herself because sure wasn't anyone else gonna do it for her. A girl who knew survival depended on getting her bluff in early.

When Macy's face came back into focus, instead of seeing the don't-mess-with-me mask she was wearing, I saw the fear behind it. Fear that said, *Man, I've done it this time. Look at the size of that woman.*

I crossed my arms over my chest and stuck out my chin, trying to keep up my bad-to-the-bone act. Then my mouth twitched. And I started to laugh.

Laughter spread through the room like rain that starts as a sprinkle and grows to a downpour. It was mostly mine at first, and then, one by one, the others joined in. Between laughs they shouted at Macy: "Hey, girl, get down from there, before you break your fool neck" and "You're about to get the whoopin' of your life."

Macy wasn't stupid. She knew she couldn't fight me by herself, and the women's reactions told her no one was coming to her aid. The minute she figured that out, a huge smile replaced her sneer. In less time than it takes to blink, she went from troublemaker to class clown. Either way she got attention, which was what she'd wanted all along. She strutted down the table like a model on a runway, giving a beauty pageant wave to all the women as they cheered and clapped.

"What's so funny?"

We looked over at Kenneth, standing in the doorway. Next to him was the guy I kept seeing around the church—the one who stuck out like a Boy Scout at a biker rally. He was carrying a tool box.

"I got Chase here to check things out," Kenneth said.

Chase walked toward the breaker box at the back of the room, while the ladies whistled and called out stuff like, "Work it, baby!" or "You can fix my breaker anytime!" His ears grew bright red, but even with his chin tucked, I could see he was grinning. That's when I figured out he wasn't stuck up so much as shy.

I studied his back as he flipped switches back and forth. Okay, so maybe I studied more than his back. He had an athletic build—muscular arms, broad shoulders, narrow waist. He was probably a little shorter than me, but a girl who is almost six feet tall can't let that be a deal breaker.

I gave my head a shake. Deal breaker? Really? There wasn't a snowball's chance of a deal here.

~

As usual, church service followed class, and after that, all eleven Transformation Place residents piled into the van. I rode shotgun beside Regina. Earlier, when we'd ridden to church, everyone had been in a sour mood. Hot, tired, and stressed from jobs or from job hunting, residents had either sulked or snapped at each other. Now a lot of laughing and kidding was going on. It was strange how the Thursday night services always took the edge off attitudes.

I thought of how all that church singing and preaching and "testifying" made me—someone who didn't believe a word of it—feel better. I knew those people in that service. I knew the ones who sang the loudest and testified or cried the most weren't any "holier" than me. I'd heard them swear and lie and seen them steal and shoot up—yeah, even while they were locked up. But even knowing what fakes some of them were, I still came away from the services feeling good. I think it was because, for an hour, the music and Kenneth's sermons got my mind off my troubles. For an hour, I could buy into the story. And that's what that God and Jesus stuff was to me—a feel-good story. A fairy tale. As long as I was at Transformation Place, though, I was keeping that information to myself.

"Gracene, you're awfully quiet tonight," Regina said from behind the wheel. "Something wrong?"

"No, I'm fine."

"How'd class go? Any problems?"

Before I could answer, a voice came from the back of the van. I recognized it as Lexie's. "I heard about that class," she said. "All the women came out talking about it. Gracene, you're a rock star."

I couldn't hold back my smile. I liked Lexie. Guess you could say she inspired me. She'd be leaving Transformation Place in a week and was one of its success stories. With a steady job and an apartment lined up, she was another in-the-flesh, Transformation Place happy ending. Like Regina.

"So 'fess up, Gracene," Regina said. "How'd you acquire rock star status?"

The van grew quiet and I told my story. I finished by telling how Chase located the thrown breaker and saved the day. Everyone cheered. Then they went back to their gabbing and laughing.

"You know anything about that Chase guy?" I asked Regina. I wasn't interested, just curious.

She scratched her forehead. "He's the church maintenance man, but I don't know much more than that. He's quiet and keeps to himself." She drove for another block before talking again. "I hope you're not getting any ideas. When you're trying to get your life sorted out, romance tends to complicate things."

I stared straight ahead and acted like I hadn't heard her. Plenty of scrapes with the law had taught me that sometimes remaining silent is the best response.

CHAPTER SIX

dozy—*half asleep; drowsy*
miracle—*an extraordinary event manifesting divine intervention in human affairs*

"Buenos días, Gracene. I'm Tony. Hop in."

The Hispanic guy with a head full of salt and pepper hair was grinning way too wide for this unholy hour in the morning. He was wearing faded jeans and a khaki shirt—pretty standard work clothes. But when I climbed into the passenger seat of his white pickup, spotted with primer-red paint, I saw his non-standard shoes—an ancient pair of cowboy boots held together with duct tape.

A cooler and a gallon thermos lay on the seat between us. I placed my own water jug and my lunch—two peanut butter and jelly sandwiches packed in a plastic grocery bag—beside them. The grocery bag also held my dictionary, my journal, and a pencil.

"Pleased to meet you," Tony said. He held out a brown hand as weathered as his boots. After I shook it, he tilted his head toward the back of the quad cab. "And that's Dennis."

I twisted in my seat and saw a guy who I guessed was in his late teens or early twenties. His glazed eyes suggested he was a little hung over—or stoned. Or maybe he was as dozy at this hour as I was. We gave each other a quick nod and a "hey," and I turned back around to face the front. I buckled my seatbelt and didn't even try to hold in my yawn.

Tony chuckled. "Yeah, it's early. But the sooner we start the sooner we can knock off this afternoon when it gets really hot."

After Regina told me about the landscaping job, she'd lined up an interview for me with Richard Powers. Richard seemed like a nice enough guy, and he offered a fair salary—a good thing since a hefty chunk of it would be going into my required savings account and later to the state. What was left over barely covered expenses like food and utilities.

But besides being outdoor work and paying decent wages, this job had another plus—I could carpool. A huge deal to someone who doesn't have her own wheels. And even if I did, with DUIs on my record, a driver's license would have cost me as much as a car.

Richard hired me on a Friday, and the following Tuesday I was rattling along in Tony's truck to my first worksite. Tony hummed softly and tapped his fingers on the steering wheel as we headed east. The sun had barely cleared the treetops, and already the hot air blowing through the windows made me think of the inside of a clothes dryer. I was glad I hadn't bothered to put on makeup. Sweat would've washed it away in no time.

We were the first to arrive on the site, a brand new house on acreage northeast of Oklahoma City. Before long, about twelve other workers—all men—arrived and started scurrying around like squirrels gathering nuts. In the middle of all that scurrying, some of the guys would glance over at me and frown. Then they'd mumble either to themselves or to a buddy. I knew what they were saying—that there was no way I could do the same amount of work as them but was probably getting the same pay.

When a flatbed trailer arrived with enough sod to cover a couple of football fields, I watched two men hoist three sections apiece from the trailer. I pulled on my work gloves and loaded my arms with four.

～

Me and three other guys spent the next five hours laying sod. Sweaty, itchy work that had my arms and lower back screaming for mercy after the first thirty minutes. But I made sure I matched the other workers section for section. Sweet relief finally came at noon, when Tony, who I learned was the foreman, told us to break for lunch. I saw Dennis pile in a truck with some other guys and take off.

Richard had done a good job designing the landscape. He'd left a lot of trees. I grabbed my sack and water jug from Tony's truck and took a seat in the shade of a blackjack oak.

"I see you discovered my favorite lunch spot." Tony appeared under the tree, holding his cooler and thermos. He sat down a few feet from me. *"Hace mucho calor!"*

I guess he saw my blank expression and offered a translation.

"Hot one today." He mopped his forehead with a stained, white handkerchief. Then he began pulling enough food from the cooler to stock a Tex-Mex buffet.

I unpacked sandwiches—now warm and soggy—from my sack and ate them in less time than it took Tony to pour salsa on an overstuffed burrito.

He looked up and swiped his hand over his mouth. "That all you're eating? You worked hard out there today. You need nourishment." He placed a foil-wrapped stack of corn tortillas and a tub of guacamole between us. "Help yourself."

"Thanks." I scooped a rolled tortilla into the guacamole and wolfed it down. Then I ate two more.

After all the food was gone, me and Tony cleaned up our

trash. He headed off to check on some irrigation lines. I leaned against the tree and studied my dictionary until I heard the other guys returning. We worked solid for the next three hours and shut 'er down at four o'clock.

"*Bien hecho*, Gracene. You did good today." Tony climbed into the truck's cab where I was already seated. "You're a hard worker."

I barely had the energy to mumble a thank-you.

At home in the shower, I soaped and rinsed twice and still had black around my fingernails. I filled the tub and soaked in hot water an extra thirty minutes to get rid of the aches. I'd never been that tired and sore in my life. But I felt good in an every-square-inch-of-me-hurts sort of way.

～

The other workers must've been warming to the idea that a woman could earn her pay same as a man. I wasn't getting the frowns and grumbling anymore, and by Friday I'd settled into my new routine.

On the way home that afternoon, Dennis spoke from the backseat of Tony's truck. "Say, Gracene, you handled that tiller like you knew what you were doing."

I shrugged. I didn't feel the need to share my work history with him.

"Mind dropping me off at The Cave, Tony?" Dennis asked. "I'm meeting some friends there for a few beers. Wanna join us, Gracene?"

I was hot and sweaty, and dirt crunched between my teeth every time I clamped them together. I admit at that moment a cold beer sounded pretty good. But a long soak in the tub sounded even better.

"I'm calling it a day," I said. "Maybe another time."

No one said anything for the rest of the ride. I think we were all too tired to talk.

Tony dropped Dennis off at The Cave, then drove to Transformation Place. "Good call, Gracene," he said, as I got out of his truck.

"What do you mean?"

"About the beer. Not really any of my business, but I wouldn't get too friendly with Dennis if I was you."

"Why not?"

He gave his head a slow shake. "Can't say for sure. Just a feeling."

I grabbed my cooler and thermos and closed the truck door. I wasn't convinced turning down Dennis' invitation had been a good call. Ever since coming to Transformation Place, I'd spent Friday nights alone. This one would be no different.

I'd always worn my loner status as a kind of badge—a message to the world that I didn't need anybody. But when I climbed into bed that night, I stared at the empty twin and had to admit even loners can get lonely. Maybe a roommate wouldn't be so bad, after all.

～

Another boring weekend of doing not much more than chores and church made the prospect of a roommate even more appealing. I was dragging my rear back up the stairs after work on Monday, when Regina poked her head out of the community room.

"Got a minute, Gracene? I have some good news for you!"

Once again Regina's good news had been as welcomed as a cut-off notice from the electric company. When she informed me I'd have a roommate in a few days, I actually got excited. Then she told me who it would be.

I sat in a wingback chair and felt my body heating up and my head swirling. Of all the women prisoners in the entire state of Oklahoma, my very last pick for a roomie would've been *Howley-Roller* Hallie.

"You've got to be kidding me!" I half-cried, half-shrieked. "Do you have any idea how annoying she is? She nearly drove me crazy at Kate's." Seeing my shouts were getting me nowhere, I shifted into pleading mode. "Pulleeease. Anyone but her."

"Gracene, I'm not running a college dorm here. You don't get to pick your best friend for a roomie." Regina spoke in a calm but firm voice. "Space is limited, and sometimes we just have to make the best of what we get. Part of succeeding on the outside is learning to accept other people's differences and dealing with them. If you and Hallie can't get along, try having what I call 'the roommate talk.' I think you'll find that a very effective strategy for learning to understand each other."

"I don't think—"

"That's all, Gracene."

I realized I wasn't going to win this argument—not this round, anyway—so I sprang from the chair and stormed out of Regina's office.

In my bathtub, I squeezed shampoo onto my hair and worked both the soap and my nerves into a lather. The whole time I was scrubbing—hard—I listed the ways Hallie would annoy me: praying, singing, smiling ... breathing. And then there was the biggest annoyance of all—snooping on me. So far I'd managed to do a fair job of carrying out my Christian act around Regina. But in my apartment, I could be me. I could bust some sexy moves to a rock song, drop a few swear words, go on a rampage, sneak a smoke. A straight arrow like Hallie wouldn't waste any time informing on me. For the next five months, I'd have to be on guard in my own space.

I dunked my head beneath the surface of the bath water to rinse my hair. Then I popped back up like a fishing cork. I was sweating—something I didn't know was possible in a bathtub. In that split-second with my head under the water, I'd had a vision. A vision of Hallie baptizing her boyfriend.

The arguments I'd made in Hallie's defense had made perfect sense back at Kate's. But back at Kate's, I'd been surrounded by people all day long. Now me and Hallie would be living in the same close quarters—just the two of us. And, no getting around it, there *was* something a little off about the way she always prayed and sang. As for the case I'd made about her being too little to drown a grown man? In truth, I'd heard plenty of stories about people having super-human strength in dangerous or stressful situations.

I dried off, grumbling about the way Hallie hadn't even arrived and was already causing me trouble. In prison there'd been only shower stalls, so the past few weeks I'd put the tub to good use. Now my long, luxurious baths would be over. My efforts to convince myself that Selena's death-by-baptism story was nothing but prison gossip weren't working. Now that me and Hallie would be living under the same roof, it was back to quick showers for me. Maybe it was silly, but I wasn't taking any chances.

~

Regina picked up the residents from Resurrection Church on Thursday night. Like always, we were joking and kidding around. During a break in the laughing, Regina spoke up. "There's a surprise for you at the apartment, Gracene."

"A surpri—" I began all excited. Then I caught myself. The way she'd said it made me think her surprise was going to be a lot like her good news. The happy place I'd been in just a few seconds before vanished. I knew exactly what—or *who*—was waiting at my apartment.

I stepped into the living room expecting to see the new roomie, but it was empty ... and silent. I walked to the doorway of my bedroom and saw Hallie—I figured it was Hallie—hunched on the floor beside the bed. Her cheek was flat against the floor, and her face was turned away from me.

The possibility she might be hurt didn't enter my mind. My only thought? Gimme a break. She's already *praying*.

Not exactly up to snuff on my prayer etiquette, I stood there, wondering what to do. Should I interrupt her? Should I stand here quietly until she's finished? Should I leave? I had just turned and was tiptoeing out, when I heard her.

"Oh, hi, Gracene!"

My shoulders hunched up around my ears. That *voice*.

"Can you believe we're going to be roomies? It's a miracle!"

I turned back to face her, and she gave me a smile like someone would use for a long-lost friend.

She stood up and tried to pat down the curlicues of red hair that sprang in every direction from her scalp. "Hope I didn't startle you. I dropped some change, and it rolled under the bed." She released the coins into the pocket of her skirt—a denim one that hit right above her ankles. She was also wearing white Keds with white socks and a long-sleeved shirt with a button-down collar. This was in September. In Oklahoma. Where daytime temperatures still reached the high nineties.

"Hi," I said. "Uhm ... how do you like the apartment?" I asked the question more to fill the silence than to be neighborly.

"The apartment is lovely, absolutely lovely. But I wonder if I might make a suggestion?"

Absolutely lovely? If I might make a suggestion? I remembered another thing about Hallie that irritated me: the prissy way she talked. I shrugged.

"I'm not certain how you'll feel about this, so if you don't find it satisfactory, by all means tell me." She stared at me with huge, baby-blue eyes, the most innocent eyes I'd ever seen.

I didn't trust them one bit.

"I've spent the last three and a half years living in very close quarters and sleeping not three feet from another person," she said. "And I imagine you've had the same experience. So I'm proposing that we move one of these beds—whichever one you don't want—into the dining area, and I'll make that my bedroom. That will give both of us a little more privacy."

"Okaaaay. Not a bad idea. But where will we eat?"

"I was considering that before you came." She walked past me and into the living room. "If we move the recliner and lamp table next to the door and move the sofa against the adjacent wall, there's enough space for us to put the dining table and chairs over there." She pointed to a corner of the living room, opposite the front door. Then she pressed that same finger against her lips. "Let's see." She turned toward the dining room and pointed again. "The hutch could stay right where it is and serve as bookcase and bureau for me."

"That'll work," I said from where I'd followed her into the living room. "Let's move furniture."

Hallie walked over to the heavy recliner. "We'd better not scoot this. Wouldn't want to mar this beautiful wood flooring." She rolled up her sleeves, and with not so much as a grunt, lifted half the chair off the floor. Muscles bulged from those little stick arms of hers.

Hallie must've noticed how freaked out I was. Maybe it was my buggy eyes or my dropped jaw. She gave me a pleased smile and opened her baby-blues even wider than before. "For someone my size, it's scary how strong I am."

She got no argument from me.

When feeling returned to my limbs, I grabbed the other half of the chair, and the two of us spent the next hour hauling furniture all over the apartment. No matter how we arranged the pieces, the living room looked crowded with the dining table and chairs in it.

I slumped at one end of the sofa and yawned. "Why don't we sleep on it? Maybe we can figure out something tomorrow."

Hallie sat at the other end of the couch with her hands folded in her lap and her ankles crossed. She stared at the TV on its stand and tilted her head from one side to the other. "You know, I hardly watch television at all. I prefer reading."

Of course, she did.

"If the TV is on in the living room, it's going to disturb me," she said. "Moving my bed and nightstand out of the bedroom freed up a lot of space, so what if we move the TV in there?"

That worked for me. Giving up my long baths irritated me to no end, but at least I'd have the bedroom and the TV to myself. Things could've been worse.

~

But not much worse. Right from the get-go, living with Hallie turned out to be every bit the disaster I'd expected. For one thing, I knew for a fact I wasn't the only resident to bend the no-smoking-in-the-apartments rule. I liked to start the day with a cigarette before I got out of bed. But Hallie brought that harmless little habit to a screeching halt.

On her very first morning, she knocked—a mousy little tap—on my bedroom door.

"Gracene?" she whispered.

"Yeah?"

"May I speak with you for a second?"

I smashed out the cigarette in a jar lid I used as an ashtray and slid it under my bed. "Yeah ... just a minute." Then I furiously fanned the smoke before walking to the door and opening it. A crack.

"I'm sorry to disturb you," Hallie said through the slit, "but I thought I smelled smoke. I wondered if you might be burning a candle."

"Nope, no candle."

She gave a couple of sniffs and frowned. "Hmmm. I wonder where it could be coming from."

"Maybe from outside."

"Maybe. But if it persists, I'll have to get the maintenance man to see if the source is from inside the apartment. I'm very sensitive to smoke ... *of any kind.*" She flashed a smile that looked more threatening than friendly and walked away.

Like my baths, my days of bending the no-smoking-in-the-apartment rule were over. From then on, I'd be lighting up on the steps outside our door. It wouldn't be bad as long as the weather held out. After that, I didn't know.

From there, the situation grew worse. I came home from work that afternoon, dog tired. All I wanted was to soak in the tub, put on my pj's, and chill on the couch with a big glass of iced tea. Of course, the tub soak was out of the question. And as far as chilling ... Oh. My. Word.

Hallie met me at the door with a look of relief on her face. "Oh, Gracene, I'm so glad you're home. I've been alone in this apartment all day with no one to talk to."

She followed me to the kitchen, close on my heels, and gave me a minute-by-minute description of her day while I rinsed out my lunch cooler. She described all the fascinating events, starting with the oatmeal and toast she'd had for breakfast and moved on to how she'd scrubbed the kitchen floor. From there, the one-sided conversation got even more boring, as impossible as that seems. She filled me in on her favorite books, the kind of laundry detergent she used, and her preference for yellow cheese over white.

In desperation, I went to my room and closed the door. Okay, I might've slammed it.

~

That was on a Friday. I survived the weekend by staying out of the apartment all day Saturday and on Sunday afternoon. I made up chores to do around the building and came inside only to eat, shower, and go to bed.

On Monday, I came in from work, and once again Hallie followed me into our tiny kitchen. Before I could even empty my cooler, she started in with her "wonderful" news.

"It's a miracle, really," she said, her eyes wide with excitement.

In the short time we'd been roomies, I'd already learned that to Hallie *everything* was a miracle. Things that had perfectly logical explanations—like finding a sale on toilet paper—were miracles. I started to argue with her about the definition of the word but decided it wasn't worth the energy.

Still all googly-eyed, she went on. "I found a job! The very first place I went."

I stopped in the middle of washing my pail and felt my shoulders tensing. How long had it taken me to get a job? How many humiliating interviews had I suffered through? And Hallie lands one on her very first day of looking? Maybe this was a miracle.

"It's tailor made for me," she went on. "It's at Flo's, a restaurant a few blocks from here. Near enough for me to walk."

I rinsed out my pail and put it in the drainer. Hallie picked it up and started drying. That was another thing—she was a neat freak. I could barely clear out of the bathroom before she was in there, straightening my towel or washrag on the towel rack. If I left a cup on the kitchen counter to use later, she washed it and put it away. She trailed after me with a broom and dustpan like one of those people who sweep up at theme parks.

"And best of all," she said, "I love to cook! I mean, I'll just be waiting tables in the beginning. But Flo told me if I do well, she'll promote me to 'sous-chef' and teach me some of her secret recipes." She covered her mouth with her hand and giggled. "I love that word *sous-chef*. Sounds fancy, doesn't it?"

"Uh-huh." I headed to my room.

"And the schedule is perfect," Hallie called out right before I slammed my door.

～

As it turned out, her schedule *was* perfect. We hardly ever saw each other. Hallie worked from two in the afternoon to nine at night on Mondays, Wednesdays, Fridays, and Saturdays. On Tuesdays and Thursdays, she worked from eleven in the morning until five in the afternoon so she could attend the resident meetings at Transformation Place and services at Resurrection Church. On the nights she worked till nine, I made sure I was in bed by the time she got home—not a problem since I was always dead tired. Those were also my tub-soaking days.

The situation was tolerable, but just barely. Hallie had so many irritating habits. In addition to her non-stop blabbing and cleaning, there was her Bible reading. She owned a huge Bible with a worn out, leather cover. Whenever she had a spare minute, she'd spread that old Bible across her scrawny knees and hunch her head over it like she was memorizing every word. And she didn't do it in the privacy of her "bedroom." Oh, no, she always plopped herself in the middle of the living room couch and made a big production of it. The worst habit she had was singing at all hours. A couple of days after she'd moved in, a noise woke me up around two in the morning. I thought the smoke alarm had gone off, so I got up to check. I found Hallie propped up in bed with her eyes closed and her mouth wide open.

"You okay, Hallie?" I was afraid I might need to call an ambulance.

Her eyes popped open, and she slapped her hand over her mouth. "Oh, I'm so sorry. I didn't mean to disturb you. Sometimes, when I can't sleep at night, I find singing helps. I didn't realize how loud I was."

Those middle-of-the-night serenades occurred often, and

they creeped me out. She always apologized and promised to keep it down, but then she'd forget herself and the volume would go right back up. Even earplugs didn't drown her out.

The only extended time off we shared was Sunday afternoons, and each of us was so busy—doing laundry, shopping, taking care of our assigned chores around the building—we didn't have much one-on-one time. So, for the most part, I could avoid her.

Then, one Sunday afternoon—about two weeks after she'd moved in—I was climbing the stairs to our apartment with a basket of clean laundry. This was the last Sunday in September. A break in the hot weather had cooled things off, and a light breeze blew across the courtyard. I was in a mellow place—a rare event for me—and thinking my life might finally be coming together. That's when I heard the tinkling of a wind chime.

CHAPTER SEVEN

appease—*to bring to a state of peace, quiet, ease, calm, or contentment*
tirade—*a prolonged outburst of bitter, outspoken denunciation*
mayhem—*a state of rowdy disorder*

THE SOUND RIPPED THROUGH ME LIKE I'D BEEN ZAPPED WITH A
stun gun, but instead of going into convulsions, I snapped. In a
nano-second, that hated noise had taken me from peaceful calm
to frantic frenzy. I charged up the remainder of the stairs,
intending to rip down those blasted chimes that hung two
doors away.

At the top of the stairs, I found Hallie on the walkway outside
our apartment. She was sitting in one of two metal chairs with a
small table placed between them. Her favorite tea mug—the one
with a bird picture and something about soaring with eagles
written on it—was on the table. Her Bible was spread across her
lap. A contraption of metal tubes, colored glass, and fishing string
spun in the breeze. *Right above her head.*

"Where in blazes did that come from?" I yelled.

Hallie looked at me with something between surprise and

confusion. "Are you speaking of this little bistro set? I thought you'd be pleased. I thought it—"

"Not that." I dropped the laundry basket and pointed to the wind chime. "That!"

"Oh," she said and her face brightened, like she was glad to get this matter cleared up. "Well, I was visiting with Regina while you were in the laundry room, and she told me someone had recently donated this little set, and you and I were welcomed to it if we wanted it." She sipped her tea. "The weather is starting to get pleasant, and I thought it would be nice to sit outside some-times. Also, I noticed you go outside to smoke, and this would give you a comfortable spot for that. So I went to the storage garage to get the set, and while I was in there, I spotted this darling wind chime, and I asked Regina—"

"No," I said, shaking my head hard. "No way, no how. That thing's coming down this instant."

"But I like—"

"End of discussion," I snapped.

Hallie's face turned so red I couldn't even see her freckles, and her lips pooched out. She stood up with her shoulders pulled back and chin pointed in the air. "Gracene," she said in a squeaky but firm voice, "I can see you're upset. I think we need to have a roommate talk. Let me know when you've calmed down, and we'll discuss this rationally." She gathered up her Bible and her mug and walked into the apartment.

Well, I certainly hadn't expected that. In most of our argu-ments, Hallie went out of her way to appease me. Why had she decided to grow a spine about this one? I sat on the top step and imitated her. *Need to have a roommate talk. We'll discuss this ratio-nally.* I fumed for a while, then went inside and returned to the step with my cigarettes. I folded my arms across my knees and rested my head on them. How much more of this could I take? Five feet above me, the wind chime twirled and clinked like it was enjoying a good joke at my expense. I jumped up and yanked it from its hanger.

There could be no compromise here. Over the past weeks, I'd learned to tune out the noise of the wind chimes down the way, but this one was right outside my door. It would be a constant reminder of my nightmare. The wind chime had to go.

I took the hated noise-maker downstairs and pitched it in the dumpster behind our building.

~

As soon as Tony dropped me off on Monday afternoon, I made a beeline to Regina's office. She had her back to the door and was typing on her keyboard.

"I told you this would never work," I said to the back of her head.

She swiveled around. "Excuse me?"

I plopped myself into one of the wingbacks. "Hallie and me. It's not a good fit."

Regina reached for her packet of nicotine gum and tore in to it. "Okay. What's going on?"

For the next half hour, I explained the ways Hallie had screwed up my life since moving in. I started with the nonstop yakking, the picking up after me, and the singing and ended with the wind chime issue. I left out the part about being afraid to take a bath. I'd never be able to explain that.

When I finished my tirade, Regina sat very still and stared at me. "So let me get this straight," she said at last. "*You* threw *Hallie's* wind chime into the trash, and *you're* in here complaining about *her?*"

I gripped the arms of the chair. Maybe I hadn't made my case clear enough. "You don't understa—"

"No, Gracene." Regina's hand flew up in a stop-right-there signal. "*You* don't understand. I get a lot of roommate complaints in here: He uses my toothbrush, she borrows my underwear, he's not too regular about bathing. Sorry, but yours is small potatoes."

I drummed my fingers on the arm of the chair and didn't bother to count. "But—"

"If I switched roommates every time someone requested it, this place would be like fruit-basket-turn-over. I seldom make changes even when complaints are legit. I'm sure not going to switch because someone likes to talk or is a neat freak." She turned back to her computer and began typing.

I did a lot of loud breathing and mumbling as I snatched up my cooler and thermos to leave. At the door, I whirled around. "And another thing—"

Her arm shot up again. "Talk to the hand, Gracene."

I stormed out of the community room and grumbled under my breath all the way across the courtyard. I grumbled as I stomped up the steps to our apartment. At the top of the stairs, a cuss word—a loud one that came from me—interrupted my grumbling.

Right outside our door, the wind chime twirled in the breeze.

Usually on Monday nights, I was in bed and asleep—or at least pretending to be asleep—by the time Hallie got home. But not that Monday night. Hallie gave a start when she walked through the door and found me sitting on the couch.

"Been doing a little dumpster diving, Hallie?" The chime clinked and clattered as I held it up by its loop.

Pink splotches spread up her neck to her face, but she pulled herself to her full five feet. "Good evening, Gracene. If you'll excuse me, I'm going to eat *my* dinner now." She walked right past me and made her way to the kitchen, carrying two plastic bags. The lingering aroma of fried chicken made my stomach growl.

Almost every evening Hallie brought home leftovers from Flo's that she shared with me. If I was asleep when she came in, they'd be my lunch the next day or dinner the following evening. Since she'd been working there, I'd chowed down on the best food I'd eaten in my entire life: meatloaf, pot roast, yeast rolls, homemade pies and cakes ... Her comment about "*my* dinner" left no doubt there'd be no more sharing. Just thinking about all those goodies I'd be missing out on made my mouth water. My eyes might've watered a little, too.

But I didn't cave in. I walked to my bedroom with the clear purpose of putting the wind chime problem to rest once and for all. Hallie had rescued it today, but she wouldn't do it again. She'd never find it on the overhead shelf in my closet. Stuffed way back in the corner. Underneath a stack of T-shirts.

On Thursday afternoon, I sat in Regina's office like a trouble-maker who'd been called to the principal's office—a situation I was very familiar with. The wind-chime war was now in its fifth day, and according to Regina, was taking up a lot of her valuable time. Hallie had been to see her twice, in tears both times. Also, other residents who'd heard Hallie's version of the story had been in to plead her case.

Regina sat in her chair and chomped her gum. I sat in the wingback and glared at her.

"So why don't you have it?" she said at last.

"Have what?"

"The roommate talk. Like Hallie suggested in the first place."

I crossed my arms over my chest. "Why should I be the one to give in?"

Regina chomped harder. "I'm not talking about giving in, Gracene. I'm talking about talking. Communicating."

"A new roomie would be a better solution," I grumbled,

although at that point I wasn't so sure. Besides craving decent meals, I was missing Hallie picking up after me.

"A different person won't solve your problems," she said. "Trust me, everyone ... *we all* have issues. There is no perfect roommate."

After another drawn-out silence, she spoke. "Can't say for sure, but your reaction to that wind chime seems a little extreme. Like there's more going on than the fact they're annoying."

I sat taller in the chair and turned my face away from her.

"Maybe Hallie has some things going on, too," she continued. "Maybe what you find annoying, she finds pleasing. Maybe what brings you pain brings her comfort." Regina leaned forward. "Look at me, Gracene." She hiked her eyebrows high on her forehead and stared at me with wide-open eyes. "Talk to her."

~

That evening, for the third day in a row, I ate left-over pizza for dinner while Hallie scarfed down lasagna, garlic bread, and a slice of chocolate pie. She'd prayed over it a long time but hadn't offered to share so much as a crumb with me.

We got ready for church in silence and rode all the way there without a single word between us. Wouldn't you know it? That night the lesson was on the importance of communication.

I realized just by being at Transformation Place, I was putting on an act. It didn't bother me, though. I considered it survival. But that night, for the first time, I felt like a big hypocrite. Here I was helping with a lesson on "honest dialogue," while me and my roomie hadn't said five words to each other in almost a week. And to top it off, I had to sit through a sermon on forgiveness. Talk about piling on.

Back in the apartment, I was in bed by nine, but I wasn't sleeping. I rolled and pitched and tangled my covers in a wad, while Hallie rattled around in the kitchen—probably helping herself to another piece of pie. I couldn't take it any longer. I slunk into the kitchen where she stood at the counter with her back to me. "Hallie," I said, "we need to talk."

She kept on doing whatever she was doing at the counter, then turned to me holding two plates. A huge piece of chocolate pie was on each one. "I couldn't agree more," she said and held out one of the plates to me.

I took it, and we both sat down at the table.

After Hallie "returned thanks"—she even prayed over her snacks—she talked while I ate. "I had no intention of upsetting you with that wind chime," she began. "I didn't realize you hated them so much. But as much as you hate them, I love them."

She brought her knees to her chest and hugged them, a move only someone as bite-sized as Hallie could've managed in a dining chair. Her face relaxed as she started to talk.

"I was an only child," she said. "Both of my parents worked hard on our farm. We lived on the outskirts of a small town where there were no other children for me to play with. My mother educated me at home, so I didn't have any school friends, either."

I thought of my own childhood at Aunt Shannon's with its passel of kids and revolving door of shady characters. In the middle of all that mayhem, there were times I would've traded a week of using my dictionary for just a few minutes of peace and quiet. But maybe Hallie's situation had been just as bad. Or even worse. "Must've been lonely for you," I said.

"I found ways to cope. When I was little, one of my favorite pastimes was sitting in the swing in our back yard and listening to the wind. It would blow through the chimes my mother had hung from trees, making sweet, mellifluous sounds—soft clinks that reminded me of laughter; deep gongs that soothed and relaxed me. I liked to think of the wind as a person—someone or some*thing* who came to visit and talk with me." She gave an embarrassed grin. "Silly, I know, but I found a lot of comfort in it."

If Hallie thought her childhood fantasy about wind chimes was silly, she would've found my adult terror of them downright ridiculous. So I held back a shiver and only shrugged. "It kind of makes sense."

"We attended a very small, conservative church," she continued. "There weren't many children there and none my age. In a way that's bad, but in another way it helped me pay attention to the lessons and sermons. I learned some interesting things." She walked to her hutch and got her Bible. Then she sat back down and opened it to some verses she'd underlined.

Uh-oh, I thought. Here it comes. She hadn't delivered any sermons since arriving, but I always had the feeling one was right on the tip of her tongue, ready to slide off at the first opportunity. I braced myself.

"For instance," she said, "did you know that when God sent the Holy Spirit to the first Christians, he sent it in the form of wind?" She spoke like this was one of the most fascinating facts known to man. "I was only about seven years old the first time I heard that story, so it didn't make much of an impression on me. Years later, I read it again and realized my childhood notion hadn't been so far-fetched. God once used the wind to tell people his Spirit was with them. Why couldn't he still do that?"

I wasn't real clear on what she was talking about. Although I'd heard people speak about the Holy Spirit, it was pretty much a mystery to me and always put in my mind things like goblins and ghosts—make believe stuff. Instead of answering, I took a bite of pie.

She closed her Bible and held it against her heart. "Anyway, that's what I choose to believe. That God does speak to me through the wind. I mean, he doesn't come right out and talk in a voice I can hear with my ears. But I think he uses whatever connections he can to reach people and to remind them of his presence and love." She lifted her chin and took a deep breath like she was catching a refreshing breeze right inside our apartment. "For me, that connection is the wind. And that's why chimes bring me so much comfort." She laid the Bible in her lap and folded her hands on top of it. "Sorry. I've been doing all the talking. I told you why I love wind chimes but haven't given you a chance to tell your side of the story."

I was on the spot. To say I hated wind chimes because they gave me bad dreams sounded lame. "No reason in particular," I mumbled. "It's just that they're noisy and annoying."

Hallie tilted her head and squinted, like she didn't quite understand—or didn't believe me. But after a moment, she straightened her head and spoke in her perkiest voice. "Well, I don't want to cause you undue stress, Gracene. If the chimes annoy you, we don't have to have them." She looked around the apartment and gave a sweep of her hand. "These days there are reminders all around me of God's love and presence."

I should've thanked her or suggested some way we could compromise but couldn't bring myself to do it. Questions swarmed in my head like angry hornets. Why would God—who was supposed to be good and wise—use the same thing to comfort one person and torture another? And why would he throw those two people together? Like a lot of other God stories, this didn't make much sense.

"Well then." I slapped my thighs like everything was sorted out. "I'm glad we got that settled." I stood and carried my plate and glass to the kitchen, guilt weighing me down. It bothered me that Hallie had given up something she loved. But it would've bothered me a lot more to have a wind chime right outside my door.

Later that night, I was in bed with my dictionary, looking up the definition of *mellifluous*, when more questions came to me. Where were Hallie's parents now? How did a decent person like Hallie end up in prison? And that led to the question that worried me most. Was she a decent person? After living with Hallie for just a couple of weeks, I couldn't imagine her killing a mouse much less a human.

A mixture of uneasiness and sadness landed on my heart like a sack of concrete. Because I knew firsthand that desperation can drive people to do things they would've never considered possible.

CHAPTER EIGHT

knickknack—*a small trivial article usually intended for ornamentation*
subtle—*fine or delicate in meaning or intent*

I CLIMBED INTO THE CAB OF TONY'S PICK-UP THE NEXT MORNING and noticed the empty backseat. "Where's Dennis? Late again?" Dennis had a habit of sleeping through his alarm, and Tony didn't wait for anybody.

"Dennis won't be joining us anymore," Tony said matter-of-factly.

"He find another ride?"

Tony shoved the gearshift into Drive and pulled away from the curb. "If he did, it's to another job."

That was all he said, and I knew better than to ask more questions. One thing I'd learned about Tony, he didn't gossip. He was as tight-lipped as someone pleading the fifth. I'd wait and get my information on the jobsite. The men there spread rumors as thick as they did manure—which makes sense, considering those two things are basically the same.

Sure enough, the worksite was buzzing with theories as to

why Dennis had been sacked: taking too much time off, drinking on the job, "borrowing" tools. Whatever the reason, Dennis was gone.

I worked all morning, planting a boxwood hedge. At lunch break, I sat under the blackjack oak and took a meatloaf sandwich, an apple, and a slice of coconut cake out of my cooler. Since me and Hallie were talking again, I was eating a lot better.

Tony joined me at what I now considered our regular lunch spot.

"This project's coming along," I said. "I like the way Richard took advantage of that creek that runs through the property."

Tony took a bite of *arroz con pollo* and nodded. "He knows his stuff."

When I finished my food, I stretched out under the tree and heaved a satisfied sigh.

"*Es agradable, verdad?*" Tony said from where he leaned against the tree trunk.

"What's nice?"

"*La brisa.*" He lifted his chin. "Hard to beat the sound of wind rustling through leaves."

"Mm-hmm." I took my journal—which included a lot of Spanish words these days—out of my cooler. *Brisa,* I wrote. Spanish for breeze.

La brisa picked up as the day wore on. I planted fountain grass and noted the soft *swish* of the wind through the razor-thin blades. Air whispered through the leaves of a maple we'd planted, and gusts gently peppered the trucks in the parking lot with dirt particles. I started to understand how wind could be soothing sometimes. Like when it blew through grass or trees. But when it blew through bits of metal and glass? Never.

～

The courtyard had sort of become my baby. On Saturday afternoon, I was pruning the rose bushes when Regina walked up carrying a file folder.

"Good work, Gracene," she said. "If we could keep you around longer, you'd have this area looking like a regular Garden of Eden."

I sat back on my heels and studied the bush for a good place to make the next snip. "Thanks."

"You and Hallie get your squabble patched up?"

"Yeah, we compromised."

The sun was shining, and even though we'd moved into October, the day was warm. I wiped at the sweat trickling down my face with my shirt sleeve.

"That's good, that's good," she said, smiling. "I like it when residents settle their own disputes. What did you decide?"

"We decided Hallie wouldn't put up a wind chime and I wouldn't take it down."

Her smile flatlined. "Not much of a compromise. But I guess if it's working ..."

I went back to my pruning.

Regina shifted from foot to foot but made no motion to leave. After a while, her hovering was getting on my nerves.

"Something else on your mind?" I asked.

"Have some information for you. You can do with it whatever you like."

"What's that?"

"You've probably noticed Hallie doesn't have any contact with her family or former friends."

I stopped my snipping. "Yeah, I've noticed. I've wondered about it, although a lot of us here have that in common."

"Guess you're right about that." Worry lines formed on Regina's forehead. "But her birthday is next Tuesday. I've always felt birthdays should be special. I'll announce it at the residents' meeting and have everyone sign a card for her." She slowly fanned her face with the folder. "Unfortunately, I can't afford to do much else. We get a lot of folks in and out of here. If I gave a party or even bought a cake for every one of them, I'd wreck our budget real fast. I thought, you know, you might want to do a little something for her." She headed back to her office. "But, like I said, it's up to you."

I watched Regina walk away. She'd thought she was being subtle, but her message had come through loud and clear. And it posed a problem for me. Hallie didn't irritate me as much as she used to, but I still didn't want to be attached at the hip the way she did. A gift would only encourage her. On the other hand, I knew our "compromise" wasn't a compromise at all. I owed her.

When I finished my gardening and cleaned up, I walked three blocks to the Family Dollar store. Inside, I grabbed a cart and was pushing it toward the toiletries when I passed an aisle marked *Seasonal.* A red and black Clearance sign hung above it. The idea hit me that maybe I could find something for Hallie there. I moved down the aisle and checked the shelves for some little knickknack that wouldn't cost a lot and wouldn't send a message this gift was an invitation to be best buds. I was carefully searching when my head hit something above me and set off a racket of clanging and tinkling. I looked up at a display of wind chimes hanging from a wire panel.

The strings and cords of the chimes closed in around me, and suddenly I was trapped inside a dusky shed. In the suffocating heat, dust motes floated on beams of sunlight that leaked through grimy windows. I could feel the particles settling on my clammy skin. Hundreds of black spiders the size of a man's hand clung to cobwebs that hung from the rafters and along the shed's walls. The spiders made their way toward me on spiked, spindly legs.

I flailed my arms as the filmy threads of the webs grabbed at me. But the more I fought, the tighter they held. My throat squeezed shut, and my breaths came in shallow gasps. Just as I opened my mouth to scream, a voice broke into my head trip.

"You okay, lady?"

I was standing in the store aisle again. A pimply-faced store clerk stared at me with a look somewhere between fear and irritation.

"You were making a lot of racket with those chimes," he said. "Need me to get one down for you?"

My knees were quivering, and I squeezed the cart handle to keep from falling to the floor. "Nah, I'm good," I said between gasps and shoved the cart forward. In my hurry to get away, my head hit a second chime. I froze and waited for the sound that would trigger another ride on the crazy train.

But there was no tinkling this time—no clinks, no clanks, no hollow-sounding gongs. In fact, what I heard was kind of nice—maybe even soothing. I worked up the nerve to look above me.

Clay domes strung together with thin strands of rope hung overhead. The clappers were made of clay and wood. I swiped them with my hand, and they made soft clicks and clacks when they hit against each other.

I gave one of the domes a twist and saw raised letters on its rim that spelled out a single word: *Grace*.

At the front of the store, I found the clerk who'd returned to his cash register. "Hey, I changed my mind," I said. "I could use some help."

~

"Yoo-hoo! Gracene, I'm home. And I brought food!"

I was already cleaned up by the time Hallie finished her shift at Flo's on Tuesday night. From my bedroom, I heard her calling as she walked toward the kitchen and went to join her there.

"Oh, hi," she said when she saw me. "Boy, do I have some treats tonight." She heaped piles of food from carry-out containers onto plates. "Pot roast with mushroom gravy, potatoes au gratin, roasted carrots, and ..." She lifted the lid of a Styrofoam container. "Look at this. Yellow cake with Flo's special chocolate buttercream frosting."

I was so hungry and so excited about the food, I forgot about her gift. I took a pitcher of tea from the fridge and filled two glasses.

"It's so beautiful this evening, and there's still some daylight left," Hallie said. "I suggest we take our feast out to the patio."

Sheesh. Only Hallie would call a meal of leftovers a feast. And only she would think of that little space on the walk in front of our apartment as a patio. But it wasn't a bad idea. We hauled our food and drinks outside.

I never understood how Hallie could put away food and talk a blue streak at the same time, but somehow she managed it. When we'd scraped the last smudge of frosting from our plates and licked our forks clean, she checked her watch.

"Oh my, it's six-thirty." She gathered up the silverware and stacked the plates. "Just enough time to clean the kitchen before our meeting."

~

Tuesday night residents' meetings always put me on edge. There was a lot of group therapy, which Regina insisted was the best way to deal with shame and anger and even abuse trauma. Everyone was expected to take part.

That night we heard from Melissa, Reesie's mom. She'd told bits and pieces of her life before, but that night we got the full story. It wasn't a whole lot different from those I'd heard from other female inmates. There was almost a pattern: sexual abuse from a relative at an early age—in Melissa's case eight years old— and being blamed for it; repeated abuse as the victim matured; a lifetime of rage at the offenders one minute and self-blame the next. It wasn't hard to understand why many had turned to hard drugs and then to stealing to pay for those drugs. The trauma they'd gone through wasn't much different than what soldiers experience. Only instead of coming from an enemy, these women's trauma had come from someone who claimed to love them, someone they trusted.

"My first prison sentence," Melissa said, "only made my condition worse. Prison is crowded and noisy, with few chances to be alone and sort things out. And I was separated from my kids." A tear trickled down her cheek. "I would hear about their problems and couldn't do a thing to help them. I didn't get treatment so much as I got 'medicated'—drugs that basically turned me into a zombie."

She paused and took a deep breath. Words of encouragement came from around the room: *You're doing fine. Be strong. We love you.*

"When I got out," she continued, "I hadn't learned anything to help me deal with my condition. So, of course, it wasn't any time before I was right back in. But the second time, I caught a break. I got into a trauma therapy program and learned to deal with my problems without drugs." Her mouth formed a slight smile. "I also started attending church. Three years ago, I would've laughed at anyone saying this, but honest truth, I couldn't have done it without God and without the support of church people who really cared about me." More tears flowed, but these were happy tears. It had taken a lot of jumping through hoops, but in two weeks, her two older kids would be joining her at Transformation Place.

As I said, everyone was supposed to take part at these meetings, but some people—like me—spoke as little as they could get by with. From others, stories and tears gushed like water from a busted pipe. I kept hoping that at one of those meetings Hallie would "confess"—would give up the full story of her crime. But it never happened. She talked plenty about other stuff—about the times in her life when her faith had waivered, about people she'd disappointed, about how blessed she'd been since coming to

Transformation Place. But when it came to talking about her crime or how her boyfriend died, she was a regular clam. I suspected that just like me she wasn't sharing her biggest and most painful secret.

That night, the meeting ended on a happy note. Right before the closing prayer, we sang "Happy Birthday" to Hallie, and Regina gave her the card signed by all the residents.

"Oh, my goodness!" She beamed, like she'd just been handed an Oscar. Her hands shook as she opened the card. She went on and on about how pretty it was, and when she read the personal notes some of the residents had scribbled inside, her eyes watered. "Thank you, thank you," she said and wiped away her tears. "This is so special to me. You have no idea."

Some of the other residents sniffed and grew teary-eyed along with her. I couldn't help but think it seemed like an awful big fuss to make over a piddling birthday card.

～

In our apartment, Hallie went straight to the hutch in her makeshift bedroom. She pushed around books and a few gewgaws on one of the shelves to make room for the card. When she stood back to admire it, I rolled my eyes.

"I saw that, Gracene," she said, half scolding, half teasing. She made a quarter-inch adjustment to the card. "There's enough cake left over for each of us to have a bedtime snack. Let's put on our pajamas first, so we can eat in comfort."

"Good idea." In my bedroom, I changed into the T-shirt and boxers I slept in. Then I grabbed the gift bag with her present and joined her in the living room. She was wearing her long granny gown with the pink rosebuds and had already placed two plates of cake and glasses of milk on the table. I sat down and held out the bag.

"For me?" Her face lit up like she'd won the grand prize on a game show. "I can't believe this! I've never felt so special!"

I'm pretty sure she wasn't faking her excitement. I hoped she wouldn't be too disappointed when she found out her gift wasn't a cruise or the keys to a new car.

She carefully pulled tissue paper from the bag and lifted out the wind chime. "Oh my." She held it by the loop and let it twirl. The clay and wooden clappers made their soft clicks as they hit against each other. "I have never had anything so beautiful," she whispered, almost like she was praying. She went on and on about it, while I slid lower in my chair. You would've thought I'd given her a piece of diamond jewelry, not a doodad from the Dollar Store. And one on clearance, at that.

The entire time we ate our cake, she fussed with the wind chime, straightening the strings, arranging and re-arranging the clappers. She ran her fingertips over the raised letters on the dome's rim. "*Grace*," she said. "How perfect."

"It's not a big deal," I mumbled.

"Oh, but it is, Gracene. It is." She sat back in her chair and fixed her eyes on my face.

I fixed my eyes on my plate.

"First," she said, "it's a big deal because this was a selfless act on your behalf. I know how much you hate these things." She hugged her knees to her chest. "Second, it's a big deal because now I have an additional reminder of God's presence." Her voice broke as she spoke her final point. "And it's a big deal because I'm twenty-three years old today, and this is the first birthday present I've ever received."

CHAPTER NINE

materialize—*to come into perceptible existence; appear*
grimace—*a facial expression, often ugly or contorted, that indicates disapproval, pain, etc.*

HAD I HEARD HER RIGHT?

I raised my eyes to meet Hallie's. "Never got a birthday present? You're an only child—supposed to be spoiled rotten. More than that, you lived on a farm. I figured you for the type to get ponies and puppies and fancy tree houses."

"That's a fair assumption." Now Hallie was the one to stare at her plate as she shoved crumbs around with her fork. "My parents weren't cruel or abusive, but they were strictly no nonsense. Life was about work and self-discipline and praying and worshiping. Occasionally, there were picnics and religious celebrations at church. But birthdays were about being thankful for the gift of life—as every day should be." She looked up with a sad smile. "No special presents just for being born."

"Wow," I said softly. "That's harsh."

She shrugged. "What about you? Any particular birthday celebrations you remember?" Her eyes sparkled, and this smile was eager enough to convince me she really wanted an answer.

The question was tricky. I didn't think about the happy times of my childhood very often. The good memories could be as painful as the bad ones.

"To tell the truth," I said, "I don't remember much about my birthdays."

Her smile faded, like I'd let her down. Like hearing about my parties could make up for the ones she'd missed. So I dug deep.

"Don't recall any birthdays before my fifth one," I said slowly. "Too young, I guess. But I've seen photos, and I must've had fun because I'm smiling in all of them."

I chewed on my thumbnail. "Let's see. For my fifth birthday, there was a cake with a princess on it. I remember Mama made that cake and that had to have been the most pitiful princess that ever existed." I started to chuckle.

"Aww, that's not nice," Hallie scolded.

"Yeah well, Mama had baked a Bundt cake and stuck my cousin Cindy's fashion doll—not a Barbie, mind you, a 'fashion' doll—in the hole in the middle. Cindy had given it a make-over. Its hair stuck out in all directions, and its face looked like a cross between a hooker and an evil clown."

"Gracene!" Hallie's eyes opened wide, but she started giggling.

"And that's not the worst part. Mama had tried to make the doll's dress out of pink and blue icing. When she lit the candles, the icing melted into purplish-gray globs and slid right off the doll's chest!"

At that point Hallie exploded with laughter.

While I gave her a chance to catch her breath, memories of the princess-turned-stripper cake kept coming. I remembered how hard Mama had worked on it. How she'd found the picture in a magazine. How she'd shopped for the ingredients and spent money she probably couldn't spare. She'd been close to tears when the doll began shedding her clothes, but by the time everyone sang, "Happy birthday, dear Graceeeeene," we were all laughing—Mama, too.

There'd been photos of that party, but I had no idea where they ended up. Probably under the mountain of clutter at Aunt Shannon's house. Too bad other parts of my past weren't buried that deep.

I placed my elbows on the table and rested my chin in my palms. "From seven to twelve, the parties were nothing special, but still there'd been a store-bought cake and some little something to mark the event. Maybe a cheap piece of jewelry. Sometimes new underwear and socks." I gave a snort. "Even the downsized celebrating came to a stop after my twelfth birthday—after I stole Aunt Shannon's marijuana stash and sold it at school."

Hallie's snicker surprised me. I'd expected her to be shocked.

I hoped one missing detail would slip her attention but should've known better. She caught it right away.

Like a kid begging for another bedtime story, she scooted closer to the table and leaned in. "What about your sixth birthday? You left that one out."

My sixth birthday played through my mind like flipping through photos in an album: a warm April sun, a cake with pink roses, people singing "Happy Birthday," the ruffled umbrella Mama gave me. Those were the last truly happy memories of my childhood, but I tried to never think about them. They always led to memories of what happened three days later. And those always led to rage.

I counted, I breathed, I gave my head a shake. "Sorry," I said. "Don't remember that one."

Hallie's mouth and eyes drooped. Before she could come up with more questions, I said, "Did your parents call you today?"

"My parents disowned me the day I got arrested," she said in a flat voice. "I don't see them, I don't hear from them. I'm as good as dead to them." Her face became as hardened as I'd ever seen it. "And they're as good as dead to me."

The white noise of apartment living—the murmur of voices in the courtyard, a car door slamming in the parking lot, water running in the next-door unit—grew louder as we sat there. The subject of birthdays had sent this spur-of-the-moment celebration into a death spiral.

For all our differences, Hallie and me had one thing in common: parents who'd deserted us. I considered the notion that maybe, in some hocus-pocus way, we'd been thrown together for a reason.

The long silence made me fidget, but I didn't break it. Rather than prodding Hallie for more information, I planned to use the quiet to my advantage.

The night Mama left, she didn't take anything but her purse, the clothes she was wearing, and her ruby ring—the one she'd promised me. The ring wasn't worth much, but she took something of mine that was priceless—my ability to trust. After she went away, there was only one time I'd let my guard down and trusted another person. And that had been disastrous.

So I tried to use the silence that night the same way I'd used it with Selena and a lot of people—to get Hallie to talk. Before I'd buy into the idea that we'd been thrown together for a reason, I had to know exactly who I was dealing with. I gave her enough time to tell me about her arrest. Time to confirm my theory that Selena's story had been pure fantasy. Time to assure me I didn't have a murderer for a roommate.

I got nothing.

~

No one besides me and Kenneth had arrived for class. I was

placing handouts around the table, while he went to the office to run more copies.

"It's Gracene, isn't it?"

I looked over to see Chase standing in the doorway. I'd seen him a few times since he fixed the air conditioning in our classroom, but it had never dawned on me until that night he always wore the same shirt—a blue knit one with a collar. I also noticed it had a logo with an eagle and a globe on the upper right side. *USMC Retired* was stitched beneath it. The fact that the shirt was always tucked neat and tidy into his belted jeans told me he still took his military training seriously.

"That's me," I said. "And you're Chase, right?"

He nodded. He stood ramrod straight with his shoulders pulled back, but a blush rose from his neck and to the top of his ears as he glanced around the room. "Everything running okay in here?"

I glanced around the room. "Everything's fine, far as I know." I tried to smile but it was like my mouth was frozen. I'd never been what you'd call shy around guys—could cuss and tell dirty jokes with the best, or worst, of them. But Chase was quiet and polite. And an ex-Marine. I hadn't been around too many of those types.

"Okay, just thought I'd check. Let me know if there're any problems."

I nodded like a bobblehead doll and tried to think of something to say. The only thing I came up with was "Will do," topped off with a casual salute.

I couldn't tell if it was a quick smile or grimace that flashed across his face before he walked away. Had he thought I was making fun of him? I returned to my job of handing out papers, not sure why that question bothered me.

Class went smooth that night—well, as smooth as can be expected in a roomful of women with anger issues. When it was over, I sat outside on a bench to grab a smoke before the church service began.

I'd just lit a cigarette when Hallie walked up. A skinny old man stood beside her with his hands in his pockets. The way he squinted at me made me wonder if I'd sprouted a wart on my nose in the time I'd been sitting there.

"Gracene," Hallie said, "this gentleman is visiting our church tonight and asked about you."

My built-in radar was setting off alarms left and right. I didn't know this ol' coot, but he looked like bad news. Leathery skin and thinning hair with streaks of gray suggested he was getting on in years. Bad teeth, bad ink, and scars suggested he'd spent some of those years behind bars. Then I saw his eyes. A little more faded than the last time I'd seen them, but still that weird shade of green. I sat pinned to the bench and tried to breathe.

"I can't believe it," he said. "If it ain't little Gracene. 'Cept you ain't so little no more." He took his hands out of his pockets and spread his arms wide. "It's me! Del!" When I didn't move or speak, he dropped his arms to his side. "What's the matter?" he asked with a smirk. "Ain't you happy to see me?"

Happy didn't come close to describing the way I felt about seeing him. Shocked? Alarmed? Repulsed? All of the above. But happy? No.

Hallie must've picked up on my hate vibes. "Del told me he was a friend from your childhood," she said. I could hear an apology in her voice. When the music inside the sanctuary started up, she lifted her chin. "Oh-oh. Service is starting. I better head inside." She walked off—a little too eagerly in my opinion.

Del wasted no time in sitting down beside me. He rested an elbow on the back of the bench and placed his foot on his opposite knee.

I shivered and not because I was cold. Being this close to him gave me the feeling bugs were crawling all over me. It was all I could do not to slap at the tingly sensations on my arms. Instead, I forced myself to sit stock still and stared straight ahead into the darkness that had slithered in right after he did. "What are you doing here, Del? I know you didn't drop in for a sermon."

"Hah!" he barked out. "Damn straight about that." He fished a cigarette pack from the pocket of his stretched-out T-shirt. When he saw the pack was empty, he wadded it up and threw it on the ground. "Shannon told me about that place you're livin' at. I asked around and found out it had connections with this church. Figured I'd find you here sooner or later."

"Okaaay. That's *how* you found me. Now tell me why. It's been over twenty years, and I don't recall any fond feelings between us. In fact, what I mostly remember is hate."

"Aww, I didn't hate you, Gracene," he said. "Why would I hate a little kid?"

Funny. I'd asked myself that same question about a thousand times when I was little. Even though my cousins were way bigger brats than I ever thought about being, Del had always directed a special kind of spite toward me. Before I could tell him to answer his own question, he continued.

"But you had every right to hate me, no doubt about it. That's why I'm here. To tell you how bad I feel about all that." He scratched at his scruffy beard and let out a long sigh that made the air around us smell like a sewer.

"What a crock," I said and stood up. "Even if this apology is for real—which I seriously doubt—it's twenty-two years too late."

"Wait, Gracene." He reached for my hand, but I jerked it away before he could take hold. "Can't we talk? I know I put you through hell when you was a kid, but I swear I've changed." He put his hand over his heart. "Give me a chance to tell you how sorry I am."

Like he materialized out of nowhere, Chase showed up a few feet from our bench. "Going to the service, Gracene? I'll walk with you."

In the darkness, he was mostly shadow, but I could see his muscled arms were slightly flexed, and his hands were curled into fists. He spoke with a deep and confident voice instead of his usual soft one. In my side vision, I saw Del slump lower on the bench.

"Gotta go," I said. "They take attendance. They'll know if I'm not there."

"What about tomorrow night? Let's get a drink somewhere and talk. I'll buy." He spoke under his breath, like he didn't want Chase to hear him.

I wouldn't have taken him up on that offer for any reason in the world except one: He might know something about Mama. I spoke low myself and suggested a place around the corner from Transformation Place and a time.

"Seven it is," Del said, still mumbling.

I was already regretting my decision.

Chase walked me to the sanctuary, and I wondered if he was going to sit with me. Even though he made me kind of jittery inside, I wouldn't have minded if he did. But at the door, he turned to me. He gave me a flicker of a smile right before he ducked his chin.

"See ya," he said and then made a quick getaway.

~

"Sorry I couldn't give you a lift," Del said the following night. "But I had to hitch a ride myself."

We sat on the patio at Clive's, where propane space heaters warmed the chilly air and people nursed bottles of over-priced beer with weird names. The place was a little too hipster for me. I'd picked it only because I could walk to it.

I cast my eyes around the patio to avoid looking at Del, who sat across from me at a picnic table. My visual tour stopped short when I spotted a guy in a far corner. The light was dim, but—no doubt about it—the guy was Chase. He was sitting at a table with two men I didn't recognize. What was he doing here? Clive's didn't seem his kind of place any more than it was mine. What if he saw me with Del and thought we were on a *date*?! I shifted on my bench so that my back was toward him.

Del took a draw from a longneck, while I tried to cool my burning hate for him with an iced tea. It wasn't working.

"Sure that's all you want?" he asked. "I'm buying."

"This is fine."

He placed his forearms on the table and clasped his hands. His sleeves were rolled up, exposing track marks.

"You usin', Del?" I asked.

"Whadda ya' mean?"

I nodded at his arms.

He looked at them and flinched, like he was surprised to find the needle marks were there. "Oh, you mean these. Nah. Not anymore. I licked that demon years back. Ain't never going through that again." He rolled down his sleeves and kept his head lowered. "Look, Gracene, I got a sorry past. Nobody knows that better'n me. I did some rotten things to you, and I've spent a lot of sleepless nights because of 'em. My only comfort—small as it is —is that I never laid a hand on you. I might've been a lot of awful things, but I weren't no perve."

I almost laughed out loud. He'd said it like "I weren't no perve" was something he'd write on a job application under qual-ifications.

He swallowed a gulp of beer and then let out a long sigh. "A man gets to an age where he knows he ain't gonna live forever, and he wants to make things right. At least what things he can." His voice was dripping with sincerity. "And that's why I came looking for you. I can't do much to change the past, but at least I can tell you how sorry I am for picking on a helpless little kid."

He kept talking while my mind considered the claim he'd "never laid a hand on me." I guessed it was true enough—there'd never been any sexual abuse. But there'd been plenty of other kinds. Teasing and taunting went on all the time. He'd trip me if I walked by him and then laugh at how clumsy I was. One day he grabbed Aunt Shannon's old cat and threatened to break its neck right in front of me. More than once, he packed up all my cousins and announced he was driving them into town for ice cream. He'd leave me behind, chasing his old pickup and eating the dust the tires kicked up. Mama was never around when he did those things. He threatened to do something worse if I told her.

"I got in some trouble here, so I took out for California, and was doing okay ..." Del's voice broke into my memories. After what seemed like hours, he finished his life story. It was a sorry one, filled with petty crimes, jail sentences, and running from one state to another to stay one jump ahead of the law—a story I'd heard dozens of times from dozens of different losers. He wrapped it up with another apology and gave me a hangdog look, like he expected me to rush around the table and give him a big hug.

I thought I'd made progress on getting past my childhood anger, but listening to Del brought it hurtling back. I narrowed my eyes and stared into his. "Look at me, Del," I said. "Does *anything* on my face suggest I believe a word of what you just said? And is there anything that tells you I would ever, *ever* forgive you?" I slammed my fist on the table. "Not in a thousand lifetimes!"

The patio grew quiet and heads turned. I sneaked a glance in Chase's direction and knew he saw us. Him and his buddies sat up tall with their necks craned toward our table.

At that point, I didn't care that Chase saw me or what he might think. I turned my eyes back to Del and watched the veins on his neck swell. When I was a kid, his fits of rage would send me crouching in my closet. Not anymore. Public place or not, I was ready to settle a score.

That night Del's fit never came. He turned his face away from me and talked to empty space. "I guess I deserve that," he said finally. "I know years of hatefulness and nasty tricks can't be made up for in one night. Maybe not ever."

He got that right.

"So tell me, Gracene, what will it take to prove this apology is on the up-and-up? I'll do whatever I can for as long as it takes."

This was the opening I'd been waiting for. The only reason I'd come. I screwed up all my courage and looked straight into his creepy eyes. "You can tell me where my mama is and why she left."

He swiped his hand over his greasy hair and let out a long breath. "Shannon asked me the same thing," he said. "And I told her exactly what I'm telling you. I don't know where Shirley is. Not a clue. Shannon told me she disappeared the same night I did, but I guarandamntee she didn't leave with me. Hell, you were just a little kid, but you probably remember we fought like two pit bulls." His forehead creased into a million lines and cracks. "Why would we run away together? Until Shannon brought it up, I never even knew Shirley had gone missin'."

No surprise that this didn't jibe with Aunt Shannon's story. One of those sleazeballs—or most likely both of them—was lying.

Frustrated to the point of tears, I tried to turn my face away from his, but it was like that watery green color of his eyes had me hypnotized.

"Tell you what," he said at last. "Ex-cons have a network that would put the CIA's to shame."

I scoffed. "A network made up of ex-cons. That ought to be reliable."

Either he chose to ignore my sarcasm or it went right over his head. "To show I'm serious about making up for the past," he said, "I'll ask around and see what turns up."

We stared at each other for a long time. My emotions reminded me of every movie fight I'd ever seen—the good guy and the bad one all tangled up and rolling around, each one trying to take out the other. Del's offer meant I'd have to keep in touch with him, a thought that made me want to hurl. But for the first time in over twenty years, I had a reason to hope I might find Mama.

"Okay." Even as I said the word, something in my gut was telling me this was a big mistake. I stood to leave. "Let me know if you find out anything."

CHAPTER TEN

heartrending—*causing or expressing intense grief, anguish, or distress*
justify—*to declare innocent or guiltless; absolve; acquit*
caterwauling—*long, wailing cries, as cats in rutting time*

IN BED THAT NIGHT, EVEN STUDYING MY DICTIONARY COULDN'T
smooth out the hot mess in my head. I was wide awake and
staring at the ceiling when the click-clack of the new wind chime
told me Hallie was home. She'd taken up the habit of tapping the
chime every time she left or returned.

I heard the door open and close and then the snap of the dead
bolt. Shortly after that, the opening of the fridge door told me
she was putting away food she'd brought from Flo's. Sometimes,
if I was awake when she came in, I'd join her in the kitchen to see
if she'd brought a good snack. Usually she had.

That particular night I wasn't up for the talking that went
along with the snack, so I stayed in bed. I heard the beep of the
microwave, and in a few seconds a sweet, cookie aroma filled the
apartment. My stomach growled, telling me the snack was worth
listening to Hallie's non-stop yakking.

In the kitchen she was heaping scoops of sugary goo onto a

plate. Her face broke into a wide smile when she saw me. "Oh, Gracene, do I have a treat tonight. Bread pudding!" She took another plate from the cabinet and began filling it.

I poured milk into glasses, and we carried our food to the table. While she prayed, my thoughts went back to my meeting with Del. For the first time since Hallie moved in, I was tempted to pray along with her.

"Amen," she said and lifted her head. We both dug in to our food.

"So what did you do this evening, Gracene?"

"Same ol', same ol'," I mumbled, not wanting to volunteer any information about Del. "A little cleaning. Watched some TV."

She smiled at me like she wasn't convinced. Like she knew I was holding something back. "We're quite the party animals, aren't we?"

Normally, Hallie talked the entire time we ate, but that night she wasn't saying a word.

"Why do you do that?" I finally asked. I was surprised to find I kind of missed her talking.

"Do what?" She covered her mouth with her hand. "I'm sorry, was I slurping my milk?"

"No. Why do you tap that wind chime every time you leave or come back?"

"Oh, that." She smiled a real smile, like she was relieved either to have a reason to talk or to know she hadn't been guilty of bad manners. "Remember how the wind chimes at home always reminded me of God's presence? Well, there's that. But there's another reason. Not long ago I discovered a verse in my Bible reading that really spoke to me."

Her face told me she was waiting for me to ask what it was, but learning a new Bible verse was low on my list of things to do that night. I shoved a bite of pudding into my mouth.

I should've known my silence wouldn't discourage her. She retrieved her Bible from her bureau and laid it on the table. "Let's see ..." The thin pages crinkled like tissue paper as she turned them. "Here it is. Psalms 121:8. I love the Psalms, don't you? 'The Lord will watch over your coming and going both now and forever more.'" She placed her hand on top of the open Bible. "Isn't that reassuring? I tap the chime every time I leave or return to remind me of this verse. It makes me feel so ... I don't know ... free?"

Last thing I wanted was to get into a Bible discussion with Hallie, but I was curious. "Seems to me the idea of someone spying on your every move would make you feel anything but free. One of the things I hated most about prison was constantly being watched."

She nodded. "I hated that, too. And, believe me, I had that situation long before I ever went to prison. But there's a difference between being watched and being 'watched over.' Being *watched* means the same to me as it does to you. That someone is constantly hovering to make sure I don't mess up and to deliver consequences when I do. Being *watched over* suggests something entirely different." Peace settled over her face. "It tells me someone—*God*—is protecting me. And that protection gives me freedom to live my life without worrying about what might happen."

I stared at her, trying to decide whether to ask my next question.

She grinned as her face turned red. "What?"

"Nothing. Just wondering."

"Wondering ...?"

"How can you be so sure? After everything you've been through—prison, your family deserting you—how can you be so certain about God?"

As soon as the words were out of my mouth, I realized I'd shown my hand. If Hallie didn't know before I was putting on an act, she surely knew it now.

She didn't act shocked or surprised. She assumed her favorite position—knees tucked, arms wrapped around them—and spoke in a steady voice. "My faith is strong precisely *because* of those things. Crazy, I know, but faith seldom makes sense in the world's eyes.

"In my childhood, there was a lot about God—a lot of Bible reading, a lot of church sermons, a lot of scripture memorization. I believed the Bible stories the same way other kids believed in fairy tales. In my closed, protected little world, my childish faith had never been truly tested. And then I landed in prison." She closed her eyes and drew in a deep breath. "I had never known so much hate existed in the world. For no reason I could determine, women who were complete strangers despised me. I was constantly looking over my shoulder, afraid to be out of sight of the guards, afraid to take a shower. I'd lie awake for nights at a time waiting for someone to carry out the threats they'd whispered during the day."

I knew exactly where she was coming from. "Being locked up with a bunch of angry, desperate people is scary, alright," I said.

Hallie shook her head. "I'd never experienced such hopelessness. But strange as it may seem, my despair—the kind that pushes you to your breaking point—didn't come from steel bars or people. It came from my mind. Guilt can be the most formidable prison of all."

I was ashamed to use this moment to fish for information about her boyfriend's death. But I couldn't let this opportunity slip by. "Guilt? About what?"

She hesitated before speaking. "Guilt from being headstrong, from making poor choices ... from taking part in a rebellious act that ended a young man's life."

Here it comes, I thought. But instead of excitement a sinking feeling came over me. In spite of my suspicions about Hallie, she'd become the closest thing to a friend I'd ever had. For weeks I'd been dead set on finding out the truth about her boyfriend's death, but when it came right down to it, I wasn't sure I wanted to know.

"After being in prison for two weeks," she said, "I lay in my bunk one night, tossing and turning. My cell was sweltering, and my mind was as restless as my body." She sucked in a ragged breath. "As far back as I could remember, I'd longed for freedom, and at that point, I couldn't have been further from it both in my mind and my circumstances. I'd reached rock bottom, the end of that proverbial rope we always hear about. If it had been a real rope, I would've tied it around my neck."

She stared into space. "Have you ever been in that dark place, Gracene?" she whispered. "Ever thought you were so awful you didn't deserve to go on living? Not even sure you wanted to?"

Oh, yeah. I'd been in that place. Many times. I thought about the day Aunt Shannon told me Mama had "run out" on me. Those were the exact words she'd used. I remembered being teased at school about my size and my clothes, being stuck in juvie for shoplifting. Aunt Shannon had left me in there for three days to "teach me a lesson." Most of all, I remembered walking out of a clinic and wondering if I would ever go through another day without feeling like a part of me was missing.

"That night, all of a sudden a crazy thing happened." Hallie straightened in her chair and her eyes grew big. "In fact, it was a miracle."

There it was again. I didn't believe in God, much less miracles, and I'd learned to pretty much tune out the *m*-word whenever Hallie used it. But the wonder on her face and in her voice got my attention. And I desperately wanted to believe miracles could happen and one could rescue me from my blackest memory. I leaned toward her, expecting—*needing*—some fantastic tale about an angel appearing or a voice coming from out of nowhere. "What happened?"

"The air conditioning kicked on."

I jerked back. "Wait a minute," I said, feeling angry and ripped off. "That's it? The air conditioning came on? As miracles go, that's not quite up there with parting the Red Sea or getting water from a rock."

"The AC coming on wasn't the miracle. It was the *timing.*" Hallie talked like a patient school teacher explaining math to a slow student—another situation I was familiar with. "I was lying there," she said, "miserable and sweating, considering the best way to end my life, when a wisp of cold air floated across me. It cooled and calmed me and reminded me of the wind that soothed me when I was little. My body relaxed and soon my mind settled as well."

She picked up the Bible and hugged it against her. "Psalm 46:10," she said in a quiet voice. "'... Be still, and know that I am God.' It's true. In the stillness of that moment, I knew God was real and was with me. He'd been with me as a lonely child. And he was with me right there in that prison cell. Best of all, I knew he forgave me." She placed her feet on the floor and turned toward me. "I can't begin to describe the feeling, Gracene. A peace I'd never known settled over me. I was still behind bars and would be for a long time, but my heart and my mind were free. Not even a pardon from the governor would've been as liberating."

As her words sank in, another sermon from a few weeks ago came to me. Kenneth had talked about justifying grace—the grace people experience when they *know.* They know they belong to God and know he forgives them, and they accept that forgiveness. Kenneth had gone on to say that for some people it might be a sudden *aha!* moment like Hallie's. For others, it might come little by little. "But," Kenneth had said, "however it comes, it's real."

I believed what Hallie said was real—for her. But I couldn't accept that any kind of grace would apply to me. When Mama deserted me, she left me with an emptiness inside that I'd filled with hate. I'd clung to it the way some kids cling to a teddy bear or favorite blanket, and I used it to justify all kinds of dishonest and destructive behavior. And I used it as an excuse to make the worst decision of my life. No form of grace was big enough or strong enough to save me.

Hallie placed the Bible on the table and clasped her hands in front of her heart. "That night I was so happy I could hardly hold it in. But there was no one for me to share my joy with. Then I recalled how the Apostle Paul and his friends began to sing when they were in prison. Remember that story?"

I had no idea what she was talking about, but I nodded anyway.

"All my life, I've been tone deaf," she said. "Never could and can't now carry a tune in a bucket. But you know what I did that night? I sang 'Amazing Grace' at the top of my lungs. Women all over the prison yelled and complained, told me to shut up, threatened bodily injury. In the middle of all that yelling, another verse came to me: 2nd Timothy 1:7. 'For God has not given us a spirit of fear, but of power and of love and of a sound mind.'" She smiled. "Who could've imagined that all that scripture memorizing I'd done as a kid would ever be so useful? The threats didn't scare me one bit. I kept on singing, maybe even louder." She giggled. "Can you imagine?"

"I don't have to imagine," I said. "I've *heard* your caterwauling."

"Amazing grace, how sweet the sound." She sang off-key in her squeaky voice. "That saved a wretch li-ike meeeee."

When she screeched out that last note, I thought my eardrums would bust. In spite of the despair that had settled around me like a fog, a chuckle slipped from my throat.

Hallie chuckled, too. "I know, it's horrible," she said. "But here's another miracle. Those threats I received while I was singing? The next day no one came near me. Everyone gave me a wide berth in the hallways, in the restrooms, in the chow hall. Even in the big girls' yard—a place that terrified me—no one came close. The women all looked at me like I was demon possessed, and for the remainder of my sentence, no one messed with me." She gave me a satisfied grin. "God used my 'caterwauling,' as you so rudely put it, to protect me."

~

"Must be nice to be so rich you can buy yourself instant shade," I grumbled. Me and Tony were in his pickup, on our way home from work. That afternoon we'd planted a bald cypress on what I learned was Richard's personal property. When we finished, a twenty-foot tree poked from what had been a brown patch of grass two hours before.

"I guess so." Tony drove with one hand and wiped his forehead with the other. Even in mid-October, both of us had worked up a sweat. "But Richard worked hard for his money. Still does."

"*Hmph.*" I turned my head to stare out the passenger window.

"Something eating at you, Gracene?"

I kept staring out the window and chewed on my thumbnail. There was plenty eating at me but not a lot I wanted to talk about. "No, not really." I turned to face him. "More worried than mad."

"About what?"

"Money." That was one thing I felt comfortable discussing with him.

He frowned. "Richard pays you a good wage. And you don't pay rent or have any kids to support. I figured you were doing okay."

"I'm doing okay right now. Not getting rich but making enough to buy groceries and pay my utilities. And I've managed to save up a little."

"So, what's the problem?"

"The problem is I haven't saved enough. When I move out of Transformation Place, I'll start paying rent. And I have all those fees and fines piled up." I looked through the windshield. The setting sun reminded me the days were getting shorter. "Fall means winter is coming. And winter means cold, wet weather and lost work days. Richard pays a fair salary, but he won't pay if I don't work." I let my head flop against the headrest. Just thinking about money made me tired. "I can't afford to lose a single day's pay."

Tony drove for a while before he spoke. "I'll talk to Richard. See what he can do. He keeps a skeleton crew during the off-season to catch up on work at his equipment barn. Cleaning and oiling tools, sharpening blades—maintenance stuff. Plus, starting the first of November, we get lots of jobs putting up Christmas lights and outside decorations. Talk about rich. You wouldn't believe the *dinero* people shell out for that." He glanced at me, then looked back at the road. "You're a hard worker. I'll put in a good word for you."

Tony's promise put me in a lighter mood for our residents' meeting that night. And the "graduation" party for Jake at that meeting made me feel even better. Jake had finished his stay at Transformation Place and would be moving out on Thursday. He had a good job as a welder, a skill he'd learned in prison. He also had a nice little house rented where his three kids would be able to visit him on weekends. He talked that night about how he would've never survived without his faith in God and the support he'd found at Transformation Place.

This was the third graduation party I'd attended, and I liked them. They made me happy for the person leaving. They also gave me hope for myself, even though I'd have to rely on something besides faith in God.

While Regina couldn't do much for birthdays, she went all out for graduations with fancy cakes and decorations and guests.

She introduced our visitors that night: Jake's mom and his kids—two boys, ages six and nine, and a girl, thirteen. Regina also welcomed Kenneth and Chase and a few volunteers from area churches. Finally, she introduced a new resident, Sean. He looked to be about my age and had a shaved head and skin the color of a coffee bean. He was shaped like a fireplug, and from the size of his neck and biceps, I'd say he'd put the prison weight room to good use while inside. And somehow he'd managed to keep all his teeth. With his smile, he could've been in a toothpaste ad.

Chase made his way across the room. When I realized he was coming toward me, the cake I was chewing stuck in my throat.

"Jake has some cute kids," he said, nodding toward the boys. They were sitting on a couch, kicking and poking each other between bites of cake. "Those two remind me of my little brothers when we were growing up."

I managed to swallow and was about to ask him about his family when my eyes fell on Jake's daughter. In her black hoodie and heavy eye makeup, she looked like a bat who'd tried to hide in the darkest corner of the room. She reminded me of myself at that age—mad at the world and thinking I knew it all.

"Yeah, those boys are cute. But that girl ..." I shook my head. "Poor Jake has his work cut out for him."

Chase chuckled and studied his shoes. "Yeah, well, I don't know all that much about girls."

Everyone mingled, but I noticed Hallie and Sean were mingling one-on-one in another corner of the room. At first, their nods and serious faces told me the conversation was a heavy one. Later, they were laughing.

As the party wound down, Regina called for everyone to get in a circle. She stood next to Jake and turned to face him as she spoke. "I'm not sure I'm going to let you go," she joked. "You're our unofficial handyman. This place might fall apart without you."

Jake's face turned red, and he looked down at his feet, as everyone else nodded their agreement.

"Seriously, though," Regina continued, "seeing residents graduate is the highlight of my life. As many times as I've done this, I still have trouble finding the words to express how proud it makes me." She reached for Jake's hand and clasped it in hers. "A lot of people in this room know what an uphill battle you've fought because we've either fought it, too, or have been through the struggle with you. To those still fighting this battle, you've shown what the support of good friends, hard work, perseverance, and faith can accomplish."

We all joined hands and Regina led a prayer for Jake and his new life. Then we made our way to our apartments.

I climbed the steps and thought about Regina's words—"good friends, hard work, perseverance, and faith." I had three of those. I hoped that would be enough.

CHAPTER ELEVEN

dither—*in a state of flustered excitement or fear*
ratchet (up or down) —*to move by degrees*

"What are you bringing to our Thanksgiving feast, Gracene?"

Regina had waylaid me in the courtyard. She held a clipboard in one hand and a pencil in the other. It was three days until Halloween, but she'd been in a dither about this "feast," as she called it, for weeks. At least it was the excitement kind of dither.

Her question put me in a dither, too—the fear kind. My cooking skills were limited to soup, cereal, and sandwiches. I couldn't imagine any of those would be a big hit at a Thanksgiving feast, so I said the dish that had been on my mind lately. "How about bread pudding?"

"Impressive," she said and scribbled on her clipboard. "I love bread pudding. I hope you put lots of raisins in it and make it real creamy on the inside and a little crusty on top."

"Who said I was going to make it? I want people to be able to eat it."

She gave me a confused frown, then shrugged. "Well, however

you get it is fine with me." She added real quick, "So long as you don't steal it."

I smiled. "Nah, my life of crime is over." At least I hope it is, I thought. I hadn't heard anything from Tony about the winter job.

"Well, it's going to be a lot of fun," Regina said, "and there'll be tons of food. It's fine if you want to invite a friend or two." She walked into the community room, then poked her head out the door. "Tell Hallie I need to talk to her about doing the decorations."

I walked toward my apartment, bummed out over my job situation and over this whole Thanksgiving feast business. I wished I could feel some of Regina's excitement. But ever since Mama left, for me holidays had been something to get through, not something to celebrate.

∼

"We'll work in the barn this morning," Tony said as he drove. "Give this weather a little while to clear up before we tackle the decorations."

This was the first day of my new work assignment and the first week of November. The calendar said it was still fall, but winter had snuck up on us. I sat in Tony's truck and watched huge flakes swirl past the window. They were covering the county road with a light coat of snow.

"I told Richard you didn't have much experience doing repairs," he said. "I also told him you were a fast learner and I could teach you what you need to know." He sliced through the snow like he was driving a bobsled instead of an old beater of a pickup. "And I told him you could be trusted. That's the most important thing. There's a fortune in equipment and tools in the barn."

At first I wondered if that last remark was supposed to be a warning, although Tony had said it like it was just another job qualification—like being a fast learner. I studied the side of his face for any sign of a hidden message but didn't see anything different from his usual, steady expression.

"Why'd you say that?" I asked.

"Say what?"

"That I could be trusted. You've only known me a few months, and you know who my past 'employer' was."

He kept his eyes focused ahead, as squint lines formed at the corner of his eye. "I've worked a lot of years with all kinds of folks," he said. "I consider myself a pretty good judge of character. I know you served time, but like you said that's the past. I've seen how hard you work, and I think you've got a good future ahead of you. I also think you're smart enough not to do anything to screw that up."

I hadn't received a lot of compliments over my lifetime, but there'd been a few. A couple of teachers had told me I was plenty smart if I would apply myself. Like anyone could've applied herself in that nuthouse where I lived. More than once people had told me I had a pretty face or pretty eyes or nice hair. And it wasn't always just guys who were after something. But no one had ever told me they trusted me.

I turned my face away from Tony in case a tear escaped from my watery eyes. I wanted to tell him that his compliment meant more to me than any I'd ever been given. But the words got caught on the lump in my throat.

We turned off the road and onto a gravel driveway that led to a metal building. Tony parked at one end of it, and we got out of the truck. He punched some numbers into an outside keypad that unlocked a steel door, and we stepped into an office.

There wasn't much furniture—a metal desk, a gray file cabinet, and a small copier. There was also a microwave and coffee maker.

"Is this Richard's office?" I asked.

"Not really." Tony placed a filter into the basket of the coffee maker. "He comes in a couple of times a week to check on shipments or inventory. But he has a fancy office in town where he does his designing and meets with customers."

While the coffee brewed, two guys I didn't know showed up. Tony introduced them as Larry and Martin. They'd worked for Richard at another location but were also helping out at the equipment barn. When the last of the brewed coffee sputtered into the pot, we each filled our insulated mugs.

"Time to get started," Tony said. He walked to another door at the back of the office and opened it. We followed him through. He flipped a wall switch, and fluorescent bulbs flooded a cavern-like space with light. Equipment and tools filled the room. Everything from tractors to pruning shears was either parked on the concrete floor, arranged on shelves, or hanging from wall hooks. There were also bags of fertilizer, mulch, compost, and manure stacked halfway to the ceiling. At the far end was a ginormous garage door.

I gave a slow whistle and understood what Tony had been talking about. "Wow! I never saw so much stuff."

"Yeah, Richard has lots of inventory." Tony flipped another switch and ceiling-mounted heaters came on with a roar. "He also likes to keep his equipment in tiptop shape. So let's get to work."

Larry and Martin worked on tuning up a tractor, while me and Tony spent the morning sharpening mower blades. Well, more like I removed blades, then oiled and replaced them after Tony did the sharpening. I liked working in the barn. It was warm and clean, and with so much noise from the heaters and bench grinder, we couldn't do a lot of talking. That seemed to suit Tony as much as it did me. We fell into an easy pattern, and the time went fast. In the afternoon, we dressed in the insulated coveralls Richard provided and headed to one decoration job while Larry and Martin went to another.

The sun had come out, but the ground was still covered with a three-inch blanket of snow. At our worksite, Tony unloaded an extension ladder from his pickup bed and handed it to me, along with a coil of red lights that were already on the property.

"Why don't you start stringing some of the evergreens," he said, "and I'll wrap the trunks of the bigger trees."

I hauled the ladder and lights to a blue spruce in a corner of the sprawling lawn. Before climbing it, I brought a branch to my nose and breathed deep. The smell of the tree brought back memories of a Christmas Day when I was four, maybe five.

It was early afternoon, and Aunt Shannon's living room looked like a vandalized bargain bin, with empty boxes and shreds of red and green wrapping paper scattered everywhere. My cousins had already broken or grown bored with the pile of cheap toys Santa had brought them and were whining about what they hadn't got. The overheated room smelled like onion dip and beer. I was in a corner playing with my new tea set when Mama showed up holding the shiny red rain boots she'd given me for Christmas.

"Let's go for a walk, Gracene."

Holding hands, we tromped through the woods behind Aunt Shannon's house. The air that afternoon smelled like a peppermint stick, and the chill made me feel fresh and clean—the way I always felt after a bath. Me and Mama wound through those woods for hours, until we finally came to a clearing. In the middle of it was a fir tree the same height as me and perfectly shaped.

Mama clapped her hands. "Look, Gracene! Our own private Christmas tree. Let's decorate it."

With its silvery-green needles and its frosting of snow, the tree didn't need anything to make it more beautiful, but me and Mama gathered pine cones and berries and sprigs of mistletoe and attached them to it with bits of vine. The whole time we worked, we sang Christmas songs.

From the woods came the squawks of blue jays.

"Oh, quit your belly-achin'," Mama called, and I laughed at her scolding those naughty birds.

When we finished our decorating, we stood back to admire our work. Mama was behind me with her arms wrapped around my shoulders. In that moment, I felt safe and protected, and I thought there'd never been anything so magical as that tree. But the best part was yet to come.

The sun dipped below the treetops, and a beam found its way through the bare branches. Like someone planned it, the light hit in the middle of the clearing, on the exact spot our tree was standing. The snow-covered needles shone like they'd been sprinkled with fairy dust.

The off-key tune of "Feliz Navidad" brought me back to the present. I looked over at Tony who was wrapping the trunk of a giant cottonwood and humming as he worked.

I climbed to the second rung of the ladder and attached the light string to the top of the spruce. As I wound the lights around it, I fought against the thought that threatened to spoil the sweetness of my memory: If Mama hadn't left, all my Christmases could've been just that perfect.

◇

On Sunday afternoon, I slid bubbling-hot bread pudding from the oven, while Hallie stood behind me and clapped her hands.

"Bravo, Gracene!" she cried. "Couldn't have done any better myself."

Actually, she had done most of it herself, but still I was proud. When I'd asked her to see if Flo would make me a pudding for the Thanksgiving dinner—I'd pay for it, of course—Hallie insisted she could teach me to make it. I couldn't convince her I was as good at baking as she was at singing.

"Nonsense," she'd said. "I'll ask Flo for the recipe and help you." She pretended to be insulted. "Maybe I can't sing, but I do know my way around the kitchen."

The only problem with Flo's recipe was that it made enough to feed her lunch crowd. "That's a lot of food," I said, heaving the heavy dish onto the stovetop to cool. "We'll never be able to eat it all."

"Be a shame to throw any out." Hallie leaned over the dish and took a big whiff. "I know! May I take some to my Bible study tonight? They'll love it."

Oh, yeah. I'd forgotten about that group. Residents were required to attend Sunday morning services, but Sunday evenings were free to relax and re-charge. Right after Hallie met Sean, the two of them decided to use the time for a Bible study. They invited other residents, and so far three had signed up.

"Take all you want," I said.

"Thanks! You know, you're welcome to come, if you want."

"Sorry, can't tonight. Need to—" I stopped myself in the middle of my made-up excuse. By the age of twelve, I'd been called a liar so many times I just went with it. The label didn't carry any particular shame or guilt for me because I felt I didn't have a lot of choice in the matter. And sometimes my ability to lie convincingly seemed to be the only thing I had going for me. Obviously, it didn't always work out, but once in a while it did— like the lie I wrote on my application to Transformation Place. Except for the fear of getting caught, that lie hadn't bothered me. Until now.

Lately my conscience had been giving me a hard time. It kept reminding me that Tony trusted me. And there were others. Regina. Hallie. I argued with it that telling the truth would be risky. I could be tossed out on my ear and could end up scrambling back to my old life. But my conscience wouldn't cut me any slack. It insisted I start earning the trust people had placed in me. I took a deep breath.

"I've got something to tell you," I said to Hallie. To stall for time, I suggested we sample the pudding.

"My curiosity is killing me," Hallie said, when we sat down at the table with our snack. "What is it you wanted to say?"

I didn't know where to start. I took a bite—a big bite—of pudding and chewed. And chewed. In spite of all that chewing, I could hardly swallow. So I washed down my food with a big gulp of milk. The entire time, Hallie didn't say a word. Just stared at me with her big blue eyes and chewed along with me.

Finally, I cleared my throat. "When my prison sentence was almost finished," I mumbled, "I was in a panic because I didn't have anywhere to go."

"I know how horrible that is," Hallie said. "Believe me. After I submitted my application to Transformation Place, my nerves were as fried as Flo's extra-crispy chicken while I waited to hear from Regina. I trusted that God would find a place for me, but still ... it's scary not knowing. Thankfully, for both of us, we ended up right where we belong."

I kept my head lowered. "Yeah, maybe. For you."

"What are you talking about, Gracene? For you, too. Nothing," she insisted, "absolutely nothing, will ever convince me you don't belong here."

I hadn't heard her that determined since the wind chime incident. I knew she was trying to help, but she was only making matters worse. "Hallie, I lied on my application," I blurted out. "I'm not a Christian!"

Silence followed my confession. I sat there and braced myself for—I don't know—alarm? Accusations? It seemed like an eternity before Hallie spoke. When she did, I didn't hear any of what I'd expected. In fact, the only thing I picked up on was confusion.

"Is that what's bothering you?" she asked. "*Pssh.* I've known that since the first week I arrived."

"What?! How did—"

"You're not quite the actress you think you are," she said with a giggle. She sat back in her chair, and her face grew serious. "You put on a decent show, but what gives you away is that you never seem to be at peace. It's like something is always chasing you, like you can never truly rest."

Boom! She'd nailed it. It was like she had a window into my head and heart. Like she could see all the fear and hate and guilt I couldn't outrun no matter how hard I tried.

"For me," she said, "the best part of being a Christian is that I might experience sadness or disappointment or even anger, but in spite of those feelings I can have the 'peace that passes all understanding.' No matter how miserable the circumstances or how bad I might feel at the moment, I know God is with me, and he's in control—of my life, of the world."

I didn't say a word. I sat very still and tried to imagine what it would be like to have that kind of peace. To feel like every day wasn't a fight for survival that I had to face alone.

"I want that, too," I said finally. "But I'm not a Christian. And I never can be."

"Why not?"

"Because ..." There was a limit on how far I wanted to go with my soul baring. I hung my head and let out a heavy sigh. "It's complicated."

Without a word, Hallie went to her bureau and came back with her Bible. She turned to a page with some underlined words.

Even in church and in our residents' meetings, I usually tuned out the Bible reading. It never made much sense to me. But that afternoon, I listened.

"John 3:16," Hallie said. Then she read. "'For God so loved everyone that he gave his one and only Son, that whoever believes in him shall not perish but have eternal life.'" She laid the Bible on the table. "See, Gracene. God gave us Jesus to show how much he loves us and to provide a way of forgiveness. Jesus has done the hard part by dying for us. All we have to do is believe it and accept it."

I'd heard or read that verse a thousand times, even before I started attending church services. In Oklahoma, it's on coffee mugs, T-shirts, even signs along the highway. So, yeah I was familiar with it but had never given it much thought. To me, it was just something Christians liked to rattle off.

But as Hallie read and explained it that afternoon, my heart grew so full I thought it would bust wide open. I wanted—I *ached* —to believe God could forgive me. But I couldn't. I looked into her eager face. "I'm sorry. I want this, I really do." I lowered my head and shook it. "Like I said ... it's complicated."

I waited for her excitement to turn to disappointment or accusation. Maybe she'd feel the need to add pressure, ratchet up her sales pitch.

Instead, she continued to speak in a gentle, even tone. "That's okay, Gracene. God is patient. He'll wait until you're ready." She picked up her Bible. "If you want this peace as much as you say you do, start with baby steps. Take a few minutes each day to read some scripture or maybe a devotional. And try a short prayer or two. God will take it from there."

∽

Hallie left to help Sean set up for the Bible study, so KP duty fell to me. As I ran hot water into the sink, her words about praying and Bible reading kept circling in my mind. What was the point in doing that, I asked myself, if I could never become a Christian. How could God forgive me for what I'd done if I couldn't even forgive myself?

Elbow deep in dishwater, I began mindlessly humming to take my mind off my worries. The tune put me in a more restful place, and that's when I realized it was a song Mama used to sing to me.

The words started coming back to me little by little: "When peace like a river ... when sorrows like sea billows roll ..."

As far as I knew, Mama hadn't been a church-goer. But somewhere, at some point, she'd learned that song. She sang it to me at bedtime and whenever I was upset. The old-fashioned words didn't make much sense, but the beautiful melody always calmed me.

As I sang, a memory came to me—one from so long ago, I wasn't sure if the details were real or if I was imagining half of them. A spring storm had rolled in during the night. Thunder boomed and lightning lit up the room I shared with Beth Ann and Cindy. Right before she'd fallen asleep, Beth Ann had told me a story about ghosts who stole little kids from their beds and carried them into the woods. I listened to the wind screeching like owls and pictured those ghosts circling Aunt Shannon's creaky old house. I ran to Mama's bedroom, shaking with fear.

"It's okay, Gracene," Mama cooed. "Just an Oklahoma thunderstorm. They always sound meaner than they really are." She held back the covers and motioned for me to join her in her twin-sized bed. She snuggled against me and placed her lips close to my ear. "You're my strong, brave, beautiful girl," she whispered. Then, with a slight twang, she began the closest thing she knew to a lullaby. When she came to the phrase "It is well," she taught me to echo the words while she held the last note. Before long I drifted off to the sound of Mama's steady, true voice singing, "It is well, it is well with my soul."

I was singing those same words and drying a pot when banging on the door caused me to jump a foot off the floor.

CHAPTER TWELVE

fledgling—*young, new, or inexperienced*
gobsmacked—*utterly astonished; astounded*
ruckus—*noisy commotion*

"DEL. WHAT ARE YOU DOING HERE?" I STOOD IN THE DOORWAY AND didn't try to hide my disgust.

"Well, nice to see you, too, Gracene." He took a drag on his cigarette. "I'd think you could work up a bigger welcome for someone who's bringing good news." He threw his cigarette stub on the concrete, not even bothering to stomp it out. "You gonna ask me in?"

The last thing I wanted was Del in my apartment, but the words "good news" had me hooked. I opened the door wide enough for him to step through.

He sat on the edge of the recliner, while I stood close to the door. Wasn't smart to get too comfortable with Del around.

"Pretty nice digs you got here," he said. He looked around our living room and nodded his approval. "Might be worth going to all those church meetings." He raised his nose and took a couple of sniffs. "And what's that smell?"

"Bread pudding."

His eyes lit up. "Aw, man, I love that stuff. Can I have some?"

"No."

He shoved back into the recliner, letting his greasy hair rub against the headrest. I cringed and made a note to disinfect that chair when he left.

"Well, just to show you what a good guy I am," he said, "I'm gonna tell you my news even with you being so rude to me."

He paused. I guessed he was waiting for me to ask, but I wasn't about to let him know I was anxious to hear what he had to say.

"I got a lead on your mama." His gap-toothed smile told me he was real proud of himself.

"A lead? That's it?"

The smile faded. "Listen, Gracene. It ain't easy finding someone who's been missing for over twenty years. But I been doing a lot of studyin' on this and remembered Shirley always said she would like to live in LA."

"She did? I don't remember her ever saying that."

"Yeah, she said it all the time." He sounded irritated. Like I was some kind of dummy for not knowing that.

"She wanted to be an actress," he said. "It made sense, her being such a looker and all. So I called a buddy of mine out there and gave him as good a description as I could. Shirley would've changed a lot over twenty or so years, but certain things don't change like, uhm, how small she was and the color of her eyes."

"And there was a ring," I said, getting more excited than I wanted to. I took a seat on the couch. "A ruby ring she never took off. She might still wear it."

Del took a pencil and a beat-up notepad out of his pocket of his flannel shirt. He scribbled something down like a detective in an old television show. "I'll pass that on." He raised the pencil in the air and shook it. "And, you know, she had that little brown mole up by her left eye."

"I don't remember that, either." I was getting upset by how much I'd forgotten.

"My friend said he thought he saw someone like her a couple of years ago working in a diner. Said she's probably moved on by now, but he'll check with the owners. They might know where she went."

"Kind of a long shot, Del." I kept my voice calm, even though a sledge hammer was doing a demolition job on the inside of my chest.

"Take it easy, girl. These things take time. Something'll turn up if we just keep after it."

I heard the click-clack of the wind chime. A second later, Hallie walked in carrying the empty bread pudding dish and her Bible.

"Gracene, everyone raved—Oh! I'm sorry. I didn't realize you had company."

"Del was just leaving," I said, as I stood.

Hallie smiled at Del. "Are you a friend of Gracene's?"

"Don't you remember?" I asked. "You brought him to me that night at church. He's an old ... acquaintance from my childhood."

She snapped her fingers. "Oh, of course!" Always Miss Politeness, she held out her right hand to him. "I'm sorry I didn't recognize you. It was growing dark that night and ..." She shrugged. "Please forgive me."

Del gawked at her like she must've come from another planet. Obviously he wasn't used to people with manners. Or people carrying Bibles.

"Good to see ya," he mumbled. He stood and gave her fingertips a wimpy shake. "I'll get back to you with that information, Gracene." He turned and and shot out the door but not so fast that I didn't notice his shirttail was caught on a hunk of steel-gray metal, tucked in the waistband of his jeans.

My mind whirled as I tried to make sense of what I'd seen. *Was that a gun? In our apartment?*

I looked at Hallie. Her dropped jaw and white-as-a-sheet face told me it was.

Without a word, she took the dish to the kitchen and put her Bible away. Then she re-joined me in the living room, where I was furiously wiping down the recliner with Lysol. Like she was in a trance, she lowered herself to the couch. Her voice came out even squeakier than usual and with a quiver. "Gracene, about this friend."

I'd never seen her this rattled. She deserved an explanation.

"He's not a friend," I said and took a seat on the recliner, praying I'd gotten rid of all the germs. I told her how Del had tormented me when I was a kid and how much Mama had hated him. Then I told her about Mama leaving three days after my sixth birthday. From there, my story kind of flowed into how I'd moved on from being a picked-on kid to being a fledgling thief and pot smoker. That led to describing my teen years in and out of foster homes and juvie. By the time I finished, Hallie knew all about my sordid past. Or almost all of it.

I looked down at my hands and saw my fingers had turned white from gripping the cleaning rag. Hallie was the closest friend I'd ever had. Would my oversharing drive her away? I kept my head lowered and prepared myself for her words of shock or disgust. But those words never came. Instead, she slipped her hand over mine and gave it a tight squeeze with her bony little fingers.

$\sim$

Before work the next morning, I showed up in Regina's office. Still on my trust-earning mission, I was determined to come clean with her about my non-Christian status. I was sweating and not because of the layers of clothes I wore. If Regina kicked me out of Transformation Place, I'd be on the street. Not a good place with winter coming on.

Regina didn't show any signs of surprise or shock at my confession. Turned out Hallie was right—my acting wasn't that good.

"I had my doubts right from our first interview," Regina said from her swivel chair. "And when I read your application—all that stuff about reading the Bible and praying every day and being 'most happy when I am in touch with God'—I almost laughed out loud." She chuckled. "I told myself, dang, this girl isn't applying for an apartment. She's applying for sainthood."

I stared at my work boots and felt my face turning red. "So if you knew, why did you okay my application?"

"Because of Hallie."

My head jerked up. "Hallie?"

"Yeah. Like I said, I wasn't too sold on your coming here after our interview. Remember, I'm an ex-con myself. That makes me pretty good at spotting phonies."

I nodded.

"But," she said, "I talked to Hallie about coming here shortly after I talked to you. She told me of a couple of incidents—your helping her gather up her matrix, your not joining in with the name-calling in the chow hall."

My face grew warm again. This time with shame. Hallie might've appreciated that I didn't chime in with calling her *Howl*ey-Roller Hallie. But what would she think if she knew I'd given her that name?

"Call it intuition, call it being tuned in to God. Hallie saw something in you I didn't," Regina said. "And that girl can be relentless when it comes to getting what she really wants." She gave me a smug smile. "Even agreed to be your roomie if I'd let you come here."

I was completely gobsmacked. Annoying, skinny little Hallie had been the reason I'd come to Transformation Place. And the reason Regina had insisted we be roommates. "I can't believe it," I managed to say.

"God does indeed work in mysterious ways." Regina swiveled around to her computer, her signal she needed to get back to work.

"So I can stay?" I felt pretty certain of the answer but wanted to be sure.

"You haven't broken any major rules, and you pull your weight around here. I don't see any reason to toss you out."

Regina tapped a few keys on her computer, then paused.

"And besides," she said, "I don't think God and Hallie are finished with you yet."

∼

"You can put that right there, Gracene." Regina stood in the middle of the community room and pointed to a long table loaded with desserts.

I made my way through the crowd and placed the bread pudding I'd made all by myself between a pumpkin pie and a chocolate cake. Then I took note of the ton of food spread over two other tables. All the residents were proudly pointing out to their guests the dishes they'd brought—green bean casseroles, sweet potatoes, salads. The side dishes surrounded the giant turkey Regina had furnished. I don't think I'd ever seen this much good food in one place.

After I sized up the eating situation, I looked around. Hallie had been working on the decorations for days. She'd arranged candles and autumn leaves, along with ceramic turkeys and pilgrims she'd found in the storage garage, down the middle of the tables. I was impressed.

I searched the room for someone to talk to, but it seemed like everyone was already visiting with family members or friends. That old feeling of being an outsider was creeping up on me when Hallie and Sean walked up.

"Come over here, Gracene." Hallie tugged on my arm. "We've saved some seats."

The three of us sat down at a table for six. Two people I didn't know sat opposite each other at one end, and Hallie and Sean sat across from me at the other. The seat next to me was empty.

All of a sudden, Sean grinned wide and waved his hand in the air. "Chase!" he called. "Over here, man!"

I turned and saw Chase walking toward us. He squeezed between the tables and took the empty chair next to me. We both said a quick "hi" to each other and then ... total silence. His ears turned flame red, and I could feel my own face growing warm. I looked across the table. Hallie and Sean were grinning like they'd just pulled off the mother of all matchmaking schemes.

"May I have your attention?" Regina stood at the front of the room and welcomed our guests. When she finished introducing a few of the elders of Resurrection Church, she asked everyone to join hands for the blessing.

Hallie reached across the table and took one of my hands. When Chase took the other, I noticed his firm grip. I also noticed his calloused palm was as damp as mine.

After the blessing, we loaded our plates with food and sat back down at our table. I was worried about coming up with something to say but should've known that wouldn't be a problem. Sean talked as much as Hallie did. Between the two of them, there wasn't a chance for me or Chase to get two words in. But I did learn a little about Chase when Sean asked him what he did for a living.

"I'm a mechanical engineer for an oil company," Chase said in his soft-spoken way.

"Oh, wow. Smart guy," Sean said with a laugh. "Where'd you go to school?"

Chase said he began working on his degree while in the Marines. When he got out, he finished it up at Oklahoma State.

Sean gave a low whistle. "Smart and tough. How'd you end up at Resurrection Church?"

Chase ducked his head and shrugged. "Oh, I don't know. I like to tinker—figure out how to fix things. And Resurrection Church provides me a way to give back."

I was just about to ask exactly what it was Chase was giving back when Regina stood up and dismissed everyone with a prayer. After that, people grabbed the dishes they'd brought and said their good-byes. In all the ruckus, I lost the chance to ask my question.

The pan that held my bread pudding had been scraped clean. On one hand, I was disappointed nothing was left for a bedtime snack. On the other hand, I was glad—and relieved—people had liked it. I picked up the empty dish and headed to my apartment. In the courtyard, the rumble of a motorcycle caught my attention. I looked through the gate just in time to see Chase take off on a Harley.

In that split-second, his cool factor shot from minus five to fifteen. And that was on a scale of one to ten. Then I caught myself. Don't even go there, I told my overactive brain before it wandered into places I could never hope to go. Ex-Marine, college graduate, engineer—and nice guy, to boot. Girl, he's waaay out of your league.

∼

"So how was your Thanksgiving?" Tony asked.

"Good," I said and meant it.

On the mild Monday following Thanksgiving, me and Tony were putting up Christmas decorations in someone's—a *rich* someone's—yard. For the past two weeks we'd wrapped about a million lights around every twig of the bare trees. Now we were assembling a nativity scene.

"How about yours?"

"*Bien* ... good." He patted his belly. "Ate too much."

"I hear ya."

We worked for a while on an angel choir. I held stakes while Tony pounded them into the ground, and then we attached ten-foot angels to them.

"I understand that they'll have music playing as people drive by," Tony said.

I stretched and massaged my back. "Seems to me if people wanted to spread the Christmas message they'd spend their money on food for the homeless or toys for kids rather than waste it on fancy decorations."

"Who knows? Maybe they do that, too." Tony knelt and began assembling a manger. "As far as spreading the Christmas message, these folks have put up this nativity scene for the last five years. By Christmas Day, hundreds of people will have driven by it. Most of them will know the Christmas story but not all. Maybe this display will start conversations. Besides that—" he looked at me and winked—"if they didn't pay to have these 'fancy decorations' put up, you and me might not be making extra cash."

I didn't want to admit he had a point. "Is it time for lunch?"

A breeze was picking up, so we sat in Tony's truck and ate our sandwiches. We never talked much when we ate, but as I looked out the windshield at that half-finished nativity scene, I couldn't keep quiet.

"You go to church, Tony?"

If he thought this question was strange, he didn't show it. "Almost every Sunday."

"Which one?"

"I'm Hispanic and have six kids. Which one do you think?"

I laughed. "Your kids excited about the holidays?"

"Oh yeah." He sipped from his thermos. "I try to keep the focus on the true meaning of Christmas, but, you know ... they're kids."

The only sounds in the cab were me and Tony chomping our food.

"So you buy all that?" The question sorta popped out before I knew it was coming.

"All what?"

"All those stories about Christmas?"

"You mean Santa and the elves and the North Pole?"

"No, I mean a baby and the wise men and the stable."

He washed down a last bite of chili with a swig of coffee and screwed the lid on his thermos. "Yeah ... yeah, I buy it. I mean, I don't think it happened like the scenes on Christmas cards. But I believe there was a baby. And I believe there were signs and clues that showed it was a special baby—God's Son."

I let out a sigh. "It's a lot to get your head around, isn't it? A virgin birth. Angels singing."

Tony stared out the windshield and rubbed his chin. "I guess it is. If you're looking for scientific proof, Gracene, I can't help you. But for me, there's more reason to believe that God exists than that he doesn't. And if I believe in a God powerful enough to create the universe and smart enough to design the human body, then it's no problem to believe he could manage a virgin birth." He nodded at the decorations. "Or an angel choir." He packed up his leftovers and his thermos in his careful, organized way and opened his door. "Ultimately, it's a matter of faith. And that's a decision we all have to make for ourselves."

For the rest of the afternoon, our conversation stuck in my mind. Tony hadn't given a lot of facts to back up his explanation. But it made more sense than any I'd ever heard.

~

The first thing I did when I arrived home that evening was soak in a tub of hot water. I was used to hard work, but putting up decorations involved a whole new set of muscles and they all ached. When I climbed out of my bath, I put on some flannel pajama bottoms and a long-sleeved T-shirt. I rested against the pillow on my bed and planned to make a few entries in my word journal before Hallie got home. Before I knew it, I was sound asleep.

I hadn't been snoozing long when knocking on the door woke me up. "Who the heck?" I grumbled and shuffled to the door. When I opened it, I discovered a cold front had pushed its way in while I was sleeping. Hallie's wind chime was going crazy. There's nothing like a blast of arctic air and a bunch of clicking and clacking to wake a body up ... unless it's standing face to face with a sleazy ex-con.

"Evenin', Gracene."

"Del."

He was blowing on his hands and dancing a little jig. The thin windbreaker he wore flapped against his skinny frame.

"Cold as a witch's heart out here," he said through purple lips. "Can I come in?"

I didn't budge from my spot in the doorway. "You've got a lot of nerve coming here again."

His dancing stopped. "What d'ya mean?"

"The gun, Del. How dare you bring a gun into my apartment! You trying to get me kicked out of this place?"

He scrunched up his forehead like he was thinking. "Oh, that. Yeah, sorry about that, Gracene. Shouldn't come as any surprise to you that I've made a few enemies over the years. Sometimes I gotta protect myself." He placed his hand over his heart. "I'm really sorry. I forgot I had it on me that night." He shoved right past me and stood next to the couch, his face all smiles. "I got some great news for ya."

He must've noticed I was about to explode. "Honest, no weapon." He held up his arms. "Wanna frisk me?" I couldn't decide if his smirk made me want to vomit or slug him.

"I'm not joking, Del. If you ever show up here again with a

gun, I'm calling the cops. Something tells me that could get you in a heap of trouble."

"Okay, okaaay." He said it like I was the one being unreasonable. Then he sat on the couch and made himself at home.

I lowered into the recliner, regretting my decision to go along with this plan for finding Mama. The whole scheme smelled fishy, and getting rid of him would be harder than shaking a flu virus.

He dug his notepad out of a coat pocket and flipped it open. "My friend out in LA? Well, he went to that diner where he thought he might've seen Shirley, and the owners said she moved to Vegas ... let's see—" he ran his finger down a page "—about a year ago with a boyfriend."

All my instincts were screaming for me not to listen to him, that he was feeding me a supersized helping of baloney. But practically my entire life was proof that wants can out yell instincts any day of the week.

Del stuffed the pad back into his pocket. "Anyway, this friend says he'll go check it out for me if I send him a little cash—just to cover his expenses and—"

"Is that what this is about?" I jumped to my feet. "A slimy trick for you to rip me off?"

Heat was spreading to all parts of my body, but I didn't bother to breathe or count. This rage was called for.

He reared back and raised his hands like he was being held up. "Hold on, girl! You didn't let me finish. Sit down and I'll explain."

I lowered myself slowly into the recliner. "You better do it fast. And it better be good."

He kept his hands raised and spoke in a soothing voice, like he was dealing with a seriously disturbed person. Which he was. "I was going to tell you that I already sent this guy some money and he's leaving for Vegas tomorrow. He has a connection there—some ex-cop—and he's pretty sure if Shirley's in Vegas, he can find her."

Hallie had said guilt can be a prison as much as steel bars or concrete blocks. Well, so can the past. The idea of finding Mama —as far-fetched as it was—held me in an iron grip. But I didn't want Del to know how excited I was about what he'd reported. "I don't know," I said. "Sounds like a wild goose chase to me."

He jerked his head to the side. "Might be, but it's worth a try. Anyway, money's already spent, and my friend don't give refunds. So let's just hope for the best."

"It's your money," I said, like it made no difference to me. "Knock yourself out."

CHAPTER THIRTEEN

statuesque—*massive or majestic dignity, grace, or beauty*
vile—*wretchedly bad; morally debased, depraved, despicable*

AFTER DEL LEFT, I SAT IN THE RECLINER WITH MY HEART AS HEAVY
as lead and my thoughts all over the map. A cigarette might've
steadied my nerves, but it was cold outside, and Hallie would
have a fit if I smoked in the apartment. I was still in the recliner
when I heard the click-clack of the chime.

"Hi, Gracene," Hallie said as she came through the doorway.
Her voice was even squeakier than usual, and her smile was kind
of stiff. "Pumpkin spice muffins tonight." She held a white paper
sack toward me and gave it a little shake. In her dining room-
turned-bedroom, she took her time removing her coat. When she
finally got it off, I raised up in the chair and squinted. She was
wearing skinny jeans and a clingy, yellow T-shirt.

When she'd come to Transformation Place, besides her
underwear, she owned exactly six pieces of clothing: three denim
skirts that hung to her ankles and three long-sleeved shirts. She
also had a pair of Keds that were now more gray than white.
When the weather turned cold, she'd paid a visit to the Resurrec-

tion Clothes Closet and gotten the plaid wool coat she just removed and a baggy sweater that zipped up the front. Every time I saw her in that sweater, I fought the urge to sing the *Mr. Rogers* theme song. More than once, I'd drop the hint that she might want to try a new look. She always shrugged off my suggestions with "Clothes don't matter to me all that much."

Her new outfit was very shape-revealing—if she'd had a shape. With her mop of red hair and that yellow T-shirt, she reminded me of a No. 2 pencil.

"Thought I'd make some hot chocolate to wash down those muffins," she called from the kitchen.

I walked into her bedroom and sat on the edge of the bed. "That's a different look for you, isn't it?" I asked it casually, while I examined my fingernails.

"Uh-huh," she said, like it was no biggie to her, either. She took some milk from the fridge and poured it into a pan. "Since the weather has turned cold, I thought jeans would be much more practical than a skirt." She placed the pan on the stove. "I found these at the Clothes Closet. You don't think they're too ... suggestive, do you?" She whispered the word *suggestive*.

I was about to explode from holding in a laugh. "No, no. They're fine," I managed to choke out. "And like you said, you need them for the cold weather."

She stirred sugar and cocoa into the milk. "Yes, well, there is the weather and ..."

"And?"

She was quiet for a moment. Then she stood taller and pulled back her shoulders. "And I started thinking. I never saw anything wrong with jeans. I dressed the way I did because my parents insisted on it. But they're not in my life anymore—their choice, not mine." She tossed her hair back. "Time to move on."

I walked across the room and gave her a fist bump. "You go, girl!"

We took our muffins and cocoa to the table and sat down.

"So I was thinking," she said.

"Yeah?"

"Since I'm trying out a new look, maybe you could give me some fashion tips."

"Fashion tips? Me?" I almost choked on my muffin. "When have you ever seen me in anything but grungy jeans and a T-shirt? Except at church when I'm wearing my 'dress' jeans and a T-shirt."

"Well, jeans and tees can be quite stylish," she said, lifting her chin. "But I'm talking more about hair and makeup. When you get fixed up, you look like a fashion model."

"Shut up." I was as shocked as when Tony told me I could be trusted. "When's the last time you saw a heavyweight model?"

"I don't consider you a heavyweight. You're ... statuesque."

It was getting late and I was dog tired, but the word *statuesque* must've put me in a cooperative mood. I wasn't sure what it meant but kind of liked the sound of it. I went to my bedroom and pulled my makeup bag from my bureau drawer. I'd ditched the colored pencils after I got my first paycheck and bought genuine lipstick and eye shadow. Every payday after that, I'd added to my stash.

I went to work on Hallie. When I plucked her eyebrows, she carried on like a two-year-old. But when I applied a light brown powder to them, she was amazed to find out she actually had eyebrows. I showed her how to apply a little mascara, blush, and pale gloss. That was all she needed. She would've looked weird wearing a lot of makeup. Finally, I showed her how to blow-dry her hair so that it wasn't frizzy.

"I can't believe this is me," she said when she looked in the mirror. "Gracene, you're a miracle worker."

There was that word again. But this time I agreed with Hallie. She looked halfway cute. Maybe I had worked a small miracle.

～

The next afternoon, I came home from work and climbed the steps to our apartment. At the door, I heard grunts and groans coming from the other side. Was Hallie hurt or in trouble? I busted through the door and froze.

Hallie and Sean were sitting forehead to forehead at the dining table. They didn't even respond to my noisy entrance. Their faces were red and sweaty, and both had clenched jaws. They were arm-wrestling.

While that was shocking enough, something else rattled me more: *Hallie was winning.* She was wearing a short-sleeved T-shirt, and my eyes went straight to the egg-sized bicep popping up from her skinny arm. I studied Sean's face and body to see if he was going easy on her. His eyes were squeezed shut, and his mouth was pulled back, showing his teeth. A shiny layer of sweat covered his face and arms. If he was faking, he was a terrific actor.

His hand hit the tabletop with a *whack,* and Hallie let out a victory yell. Sean hung his head. "Girl, you're killing me."

She sat back in her chair and wiped her forehead with the back of her hand. Finally, she looked at me standing in the door. "Oh, hi, Gracene! Didn't know you'd come in." She flexed her right arm, and that scary muscle popped up again. "See, I told you I was strong."

She jumped up from the table and went to the kitchen. I said hi to Sean, who was still breathing hard, and followed her.

"I brought home a ton of leftovers today." She pulled takeout cartons from a sack, while I washed out my cooler and thermos. "So I asked Sean to join us for dinner. Hope you don't mind."

"No, that's fine." Last night I'd wondered if there was more to her makeover request than what she'd told me. I had my answer.

The three of us sat around our tiny dining table and talked while we ate. I knew from our group sessions that Sean had been involved with a gang before going to prison. I wanted to know more but didn't want to ruin the good time by bringing up our pathetic pasts.

"So where are you working?" I asked him.

He wiped his mouth with a paper napkin. "At Simmons's Bicycle Shop. It's a good job. The owner is teaching me a lot."

"Great." I cut into my chicken-fried steak. "How'd you find it?"

"Interesting story," he said. "You know that verse in Romans about all things working for good for those that love the Lord?"

I nodded. That was one of the few verses I was familiar with.

"Well," he continued, "I guess you could say that's what happened with me. I couldn't get a job because I didn't have a car to get around. I was growing discouraged, and one day, out of desperation, I popped into this bicycle shop about two blocks from here. I went in to get me a used bike and came out with a bike and a job!"

"That's awesome," I said.

He looked across the table at Hallie, and his face broke into a wide smile. "Yeah, it is. In fact, I call it a miracle."

～

After the residents' meeting that night, me and Hallie cleaned up the mess we'd left in the kitchen.

"You're not talking much tonight," I said, as Hallie filled the sink with water.

"I guess I'm just worn out."

I grabbed a dishtowel. "Sean seems like a nice guy."

"Mm-hmm," she said, like she hadn't given him much thought. But I knew if I waited …

"He's *very* nice, Gracene," she blurted out. "And so solid in his faith." She bombarded me with praise for the amazing Sean as we worked, ending with "and we have so much in common."

She wiped down the countertops while I put away the silverware. "Oh, and did I mention," she said, right before I flipped the light off, "he has the most beautiful singing voice?"

In bed I snickered over Hallie saying her and Sean had so much in common.

Had she been serious? She was white; he was black. She came from a strict, religious family; his most recent "family" had been a gang. He was built like a tank; she was a string bean. He was cool; she was ...well, not. Then I thought about Sean's *miracle* remark at dinner. Maybe they had a lot in common after all.

∽

Even with the weather growing colder, I was enjoying working outside. But climbing up and down ladders to string lights on trees or attach a sleigh and reindeer onto a second-story roof can put a lot of stress on a body. On the first Monday afternoon of December, I returned from work, looking forward to resting my aching joints and muscles in a tub of hot water. As soon as I shut the door behind me, I heard the familiar pounding. It spooked me the way Del always showed up when Hallie wasn't there. Like he was stalking me.

I opened the door, planning on keeping this visit short. "Hey, Del."

I had no intention of asking him in, but like last time, he shoved past me. Instead of sitting down, he stood just inside the door. "Came to give you an update." He was acting kind of nervous, and even though I hadn't turned up the heat yet, beads of sweat covered his forehead.

"Make it quick. I've got things to do."

His eyes darted around the room. "My guy Sid—the one looking for Shirley—says he's real close. That's the good news. The bad news: He's asking for more money. And right now, I gotta be honest, I don't have it."

Even though I'd been expecting this, disappointment and

anger brought me close to tears. But I also felt a twinge of relief. I could finally be rid of Del.

"If you're asking me for money, Del, forget it." I reached past him to open the door. "So I guess that's the end—"

"Wait!" He grabbed my arm. "I swear to you, he's this close." He held up his free hand with his thumb and index finger about a half inch apart. "Sid's cop friend says there's a woman working in a coffee shop near the strip that fits her description. Seems a shame to just give up at this point." His creepy green eyes locked onto mine. "Especially since I've already put so much of my own time and money into this."

I pulled my arm from his grip but didn't walk away. I ignored the voice telling me it was stupid to give him and his lame-brain scheme another second of my time, much less money. But on the off-chance—the way off-chance—he wasn't just blowing smoke, I couldn't let it go. I squelched the warning voice with one that said Mama needed to know how she'd ruined my life. And she needed to know how much I hated her for that.

I went to my bedroom and dug deep into my sock drawer for cash I'd squirreled away for when I moved out and for Christmas gifts. As I held that money and thought about what I was doing, my hand began to shake. I'd been doing so well putting my life back together. Now, here I was, putting my hopes—and my money—into the hands of a broken-down druggie, letting all the sadness and misery of my past slide right back into my life.

I returned to the living room, squeezing the bills so tight my fingers were cramping. "This is it, Del." I shoved the cash toward him. "All I've got. And if I find out you've been—"

"Don't worry." He snatched the money from my hand and stuffed it in his pocket. "I'm telling you this could be the break we've been waiting for." He smiled like he was making fun of me. "Who knows? Ol' Santy might just bring you a mama for Christmas."

~

After Del left, I sat in the living room in the dark. When Hallie came in from work, I was still there.

"Hey, Gracene," she said. "Why're you sitting here without—"

She switched on the light. Instead of finishing her question, she scrunched her forehead into worry lines. "I brought some blueberry muffins from Flo's. Why don't I warm them up and fix us some hot tea?"

I heard her humming as she puttered around in the kitchen. My lips curved into a semi grin, and I shook my head. Her humming was as bad as her singing.

When she came back into the living room, she was carrying the tea and muffins on a tray. Instead of putting the food on the table where we usually ate, she placed it on the coffee table and sat down beside me on the couch.

"So what's going on?" She picked up her favorite mug and took a sip.

I really wanted to talk but didn't know where to begin. "Nothing really."

She didn't press. Instead, she stretched out her legs and rested her feet on the coffee table. Then she hummed the same song she'd been humming in the kitchen.

"I love this song," she said. "Are you familiar with it?"

I shook my head.

"It's called 'To God Be the Glory.' I like the modern praise songs we sing at church, but I was raised on the old hymns. Some of the words seem strange to people these days, but if you really listen, there's so much truth in them." She hummed a little more, then sang "... the vilest offender who truly believes, that moment from Jesus a pardon receives." A pleased smile settled on her face. "I love that phrase. It always reminds me that even though I was one of those 'vilest offenders,' I've been forgiven."

I'd looked up the definition of *vile* once when Aunt Shannon used it to describe me. The word pretty much covers anything and everything that is evil and worthless. Over the years, I'd come to the conclusion the word was a pretty good fit for me. But Hallie? We'd been living under the same roof for almost three months, and nothing I'd seen from her hinted in the least way she was "depraved" or "despicable." It was time to settle this matter.

"Hallie, something's been bothering me for a long time. Exactly what happened the day your boyfriend was killed?"

She cocked her head and gave me a sideways stare. "You mean you don't believe the rumors about me drowning him?"

CHAPTER FOURTEEN

shenanigans—*mischief, deceit, trickery*
infraction—*breach, violation, infringement*

"YOU KNEW ABOUT THOSE?"

She rolled her eyes. "How could I not know? Like a lot of things I heard in prison, I dismissed them as ridiculous gossip. And I figured anyone with any sense would do the same."

The hot tea I gulped almost scalded the roof of my mouth.

"But I should've told you the truth a long time ago," she said. "So here goes." She scooted into the corner of the couch so that she was facing me and began by reminding me of her lonely childhood. "When I was little, I managed my loneliness with projects and chores and a lot of daydreaming. But by seventeen I'd developed an interest in boys—although I'd never been around many—and by eighteen, I'd grown restless."

She twisted her mouth into a line of disgust. "Eighteen years old, and I'd never been more than fifty miles from our farm. And as for guys, I'd hardly ever talked to a boy, much less been on a date. Can you believe that?"

I'll admit it was hard for me to get my mind around that last part. By the time I was *thirteen*, I knew about the opposite sex. *All* about it. Or at least I thought I did. But as it turned out, I didn't know enough to keep me out of trouble. Didn't know which guys could and couldn't be trusted.

"Anyway," Hallie said, "right after I turned nineteen, Daddy was in a bind to get a wheat crop harvested before rainy weather set in. He hired three men to help, and one of them looked to be about my age. Daddy was so busy he couldn't keep a close eye on things like he usually did. And Mickey was good at sneaking around."

"Mickey?"

She nodded. "Poor, timid, skinny Mickey. He'd left home when he was sixteen and had already been on his own a couple of years when he showed up at our place. Not very smart, but he was young and male and kind of cute—so he caught my attention." She stared into her mug. "He'd been at the farm a couple of weeks when he talked me into slipping out at night."

"So ... what did you do?"

"*Psssh.* We were so clueless. Mostly we went for long rides in his beat up old car. And sometimes we'd park somewhere and just talk. Well, mainly I talked, and Mickey listened."

While the part about her doing all the talking didn't surprise me, the fact she'd found the nerve to sneak out at night did. "Weren't you afraid of getting caught?"

She hugged her knees to her chest. "I was petrified. That was the first time in my entire life I'd disobeyed my parents, and I had no idea what they'd do if they caught me. But at the same time, it was thrilling. Almost addicting. I finally felt like my own person. I finally felt free."

Hallie was such a little homebody with all her cooking and cleaning, I couldn't understand why freedom was so important to her. But as I thought about it, I realized most people yearn for freedom in one form or another. Every inmate I'd met while inside couldn't wait to be free from prison bars. Hallie wanted freedom from her restrictive parents and upbringing. A lot of the residents at Transformation Place had fought hard to be free from their addictions. And me? That was a no-brainer. I wanted to be free from my past.

"Of course, we eventually got caught," Hallie said. "One night we pulled into the driveway, and Daddy came out to meet us." Her voice began to shake. "He yanked me from the car so hard I landed on the ground."

"What about Mickey? Did he do anything to him?"

"Mickey gunned the engine and sped away. As he was driving off, Daddy threatened to shoot him if he ever came on our place again."

I sucked in a sharp breath. "Do you think he was serious?"

Hallie shook her head. "I don't think my dad even owned a gun. But he was so mad that night, I don't want to think what would've happened if he did.

"I moped around for two weeks after that. Then one afternoon when Daddy was away, Mickey slipped back on the farm. He was driving a newer car and asked me if I wanted to go for a ride."

"And you went," I said, knowing where this story was going.

Hallie stretched her legs and rested her feet on the coffee table. "For two weeks I hadn't been allowed to go anywhere or see anyone. And my parents and I hadn't exchanged five civil words the entire time." Anger crept into her voice. "I tell you, Gracene, if Satan himself had offered me a ride that day, I would've taken him up on it. I jumped in"—she flicked her hand—"and away we went."

"Whoa, you rebel, you!" I knew this story had a bad ending, but I couldn't help chuckling.

"Whatever," she said, giggling a little herself. "We'd been

riding around for about fifteen minutes when Mickey asked me to run away with him." Any sign of cheer she'd just shown disappeared. "I didn't even like Mickey that much, but that invitation was a chance to escape. And no telling what would happen if I went back to the farm, so ... I agreed."

"You just took off? No clothes, no money, no nothing?" I'd pulled those kinds of shenanigans on a weekly basis as a teenager but couldn't imagine Hallie doing it.

"The first two days, I enjoyed myself," she said. "Mickey and I flew down country roads like we didn't have a care in the world." She rested her head against the back of the couch, and her shoulders sagged. "Then his money started running low. For the next two days we ate cheese-crackers and washed them down with water. And we slept in his car. Then the cheese-crackers ran out. At a convenience store on the edge of a small town, Mickey put some gas in the car. Before he went in to pay and find out about jobs, he asked me to drive. Said he was getting sleepy. So while he was inside, I slid behind the wheel."

Hallie raised her hands in front of her chest. She clenched them so hard her knuckles turned white. "The next thing I knew, he was running out of the store. He tossed some snacks onto the seat between us and yelled, 'Let's go.' I started to ask him what was going on, but he cut me off and yelled louder, 'Just go!' He was turned in his seat and looking out the back window, and he kept shouting for me to drive faster. I was already so scared I hardly knew what I was doing. And then I heard sirens."

"Ooh, not good," I said. I knew firsthand the panic attack that sound could bring on.

"I was so terrified it was like I wasn't in control of my own body." She unclenched her fists and wiggled her fingers. "Like I was a puppet and some unknown force was pulling the strings. The car was picking up speed, and everything was passing in a blur. I heard sirens wailing and Mickey shouting, and when I couldn't stand the racket another second, I pressed my palms against my ears."

As she told that last part, Hallie had placed her hands over her ears like she was experiencing that whole nightmarish scene again. She sat like that for a moment, and then her hands dropped to her side. When she spoke again, she stared at the wall, not blinking. "The next thing I remember was standing in a creek with reddish-brown water swirling around my knees. Mickey was unconscious, and I was holding his head above the water and screaming for help."

She covered her face and broke into sobs. When the sobs died down, she spoke between sniffs. "I learned later when we plowed through the guardrail, Mickey's spine snapped in two. He died instantly."

"Oh, Hallie." I hurt so bad for her but couldn't find the words to say how much. So I just let her cry some more.

"I also found out Mickey hadn't paid for the gas or the food," she said after a while. "And he'd stolen the car. I hadn't known any of that beforehand, and without a witness, it would've been hard for the prosecutor to prove that I did. But still, there were charges—eluding arrest and manslaughter. Those add up to serious time—ten years to be exact. My public defender plea bargained for three and a half years prison time with the remainder on probation."

This whole story made me sick to my stomach. I was sorry I'd brought it up. "That's just wrong," I said, feeling my anger build. "All you wanted was a normal life. You'd never so much as stolen a stick of gum."

Hallie's body was as limp as a rag doll's. "Like I told you, my parents wanted nothing more to do with me. Wouldn't raise my bail, wouldn't hire an attorney. Also, I didn't give my public defender much to work with. So, fair or not, that's what it was."

"Why didn't you fight? Defend yourself?"

She shrugged. "I felt so awful about Mickey's death. Thought prison time would ease some of my guilt."

"Guilt? You didn't kill him. You tried to save him."

She kept her head resting against the back of the couch, like it was too heavy to lift. "I did. But I also played a part in his death." Her words came out slow and tired. "I was the one driving the car. I was the one who plowed through the guardrail. More than that, if it hadn't been for my rebellious heart, we wouldn't have been in that situation in the first place."

"I don't know, Hal—"

She raised her hand and cut me off. We sat beside each other, neither of us talking.

"I apologize, Hallie," I whispered after a while.

"Apologize? For what?"

"For making you tell this story. For taking advantage of your willingness to be open with me. For making you live through your nightmare all over again."

"You didn't *make* me tell it, Gracene. I chose to." She looked at me through watery eyes. "What happened to Mickey still hurts. I still grieve for the chance at life he lost, and I always will. Those times you hear me singing in the middle of the night? They're usually after I've had a dream about him, and my crying wakes me up."

Hallie sniffed and smoothed soggy strands of hair from her face. "But I know God has forgiven me." She gave me a trembly smile. "And he helps me deal with my pain. If my story can spread the message about his love and forgiveness, I want to tell it."

~

"That's it, Gracene. The end of our decorating jobs."

Me and Tony were driving home after another back-breaking day.

"You won't hear me complaining about that," I said. "I don't care if I never see another Christmas light."

"Can't blame you, there. But it's also the end of our overtime pay."

I leaned against the passenger door and fought back mild panic. In just a few weeks, I'd be completing my six months at Transformation Place. The overtime pay had helped with my finances, but I still didn't have nearly enough to go it alone.

Besides the money, I wondered if I'd be ready in other ways. Even with all the "policies and procedures" and a constant support system where I lived, my past had gained a toehold back into my life. Without a barricade of rules and friends surrounding me, would it completely take over?

~

After Tony dropped me off, I stepped inside the apartment and found Hallie and Sean standing beside a fake tree. Tangled strings of colored lights and boxes of ornaments were scattered across the living room. Christmas music blared from a CD player Sean must've provided.

"Look at all this, Gracene!" Hallie's smile was shinier than the glittery ornament she was holding. "Some ladies from a church brought it over. They offered to decorate, but I told them we'd do it. We don't want to miss out on the fun, right?"

I collapsed onto the sofa. "Looks like you two have it under control," I said, trying not to be too much of a party pooper. I yawned and stretched. "Why don't I just watch?"

My Grinch-ly attitude didn't discourage either her or Sean. They covered that five-foot tree in about a million flashing lights and made a big fuss over every ornament they hung on it—even the one that looked like Elvis Presley. I was thinking what a couple of goobers they were when it occurred to me this was probably Hallie's first Christmas tree. Could've been Sean's, too.

Between their comments, they sang along with the CD. Sean's singing made me think of Smoky Robinson. Hallie's made me think of Tarzan. But their happiness was hard to resist. When "Jingle Bell Rock" started playing, I joined in both the singing and the decorating.

When there wasn't an undecorated square inch left on the tree, Hallie held up a battered cardboard container. "Last box," she said as she lifted the lid. She peeled away some tissue paper and gave a soft *oooh,* as she took out a glass manger holding a baby Jesus. Some paint had chipped off the manger, and the baby was missing a tiny finger. But Hallie didn't seem to notice.

"Would you just look at this?" Her words came out almost like a prayer. "Who would give away such a treasure?"

Me and Sean took the rest of the nativity scene from the box and helped her arrange it under the tree. We placed the final wise man in just the right position and stood back to admire our work. I'd helped Tony put up some high-dollar decorations over the past few weeks. None of them came close to being as beautiful as that second-hand tree and nativity in our living room.

After cleaning up the decorating mess, the three of us grabbed a quick supper and headed to the community room for the residents' meeting. Before we got into the lesson, we spent a few minutes making plans for the upcoming Christmas party. Just my luck, Regina assigned me the job of putting up outside lights. According to her, this party was always a big deal. Or in her exact words, "the highlight of the year." But the way she barked out orders and chomped her gum made me think she was feeling more on edge than excited.

After our lesson on the things people use as a substitute for God—money, fame, drugs, family—the meeting broke up. I was on my way out of the room, when Regina tapped me on the shoulder.

"Can I talk to you a minute?" She nodded toward her office.

I followed her, trying to think of what infraction I'd committed. I couldn't come up with anything—not recently, anyway—but who knew? There were so many rules.

She turned on a lamp in her office and sat in one of the wing-back chairs. "Have a seat," she said, all business-like.

I sat down in the matching chair, still drawing a blank on what I'd done wrong.

"I've noticed you've had a guest lately," she said. She didn't sound mad exactly but sort of stressed.

"A guest?"

"A male guest. Older guy. Kind of scraggly."

The word "scraggly" cleared up my confusion. "Ah! You mean Del." I nodded. "Yeah, he was my aunt Shannon's friend when I was a kid. He moved back in with her a few months ago, and he's dropped by a couple of times." I saw her frown. "What? He only stayed a few minutes both times. Not overnight. I didn't break any rules, did I?"

"No. Just make sure you don't."

She kind of snapped those last words at me, and it made me mad. I had a hard enough time handling accusation when I was guilty. I sure didn't like being scolded for something I hadn't done. And the idea of Del sleeping over in my apartment made me want to gag. "No problem," I snapped back. I stood and started for the door.

"Wait a minute, Gracene."

I halted in the doorway but kept my back to her.

"I'm sorry," she said. Her voice was softer than before.

I turned around. Deep creases lined her face, and the corners of her eyes drooped.

"I got some bad news today, and I guess I was just looking for someone to take out my frustration on."

"What news?"

It must've been bad. I'd seen Regina happy, mad, excited, frustrated. But I'd never seen her look as whipped as she did right then.

"You remember Lexi?" she asked.

"Yeah. I liked her. She's okay, isn't she?"

She shook her head. "Afraid not. Back in jail."

Like a sucker punch, this information came from nowhere and left me reeling. I sank back down in my chair. "What happened?"

"She wasn't ready." Regina rubbed her temples like she had a headache. "Wasn't ready to handle all the temptation the world throws at someone when they're on their own and still trying to get their bearings. She got arrested again for drunk driving. This sentence will be a long one." She took a quick swipe at her eyes and faced me. "Have I ever told you my dream?"

I shook my head.

"I tell our board all the time that six months isn't long enough. It's not enough time to prepare some people for the challenges the world's going to throw at them when they leave here. And for folks with addiction problems, it's ten times worse."

What she said made my throat close up tight and my heart race. That mild panic over leaving that I'd felt a few hours earlier was on the verge of a full-blown attack.

Regina straightened herself in the chair. "Sometimes— depending on the demand for apartments—we can stretch the stay here to nine months. But in many cases, even that's not long enough." Her face took on a determined look, and I heard the familiar hope return to her voice. "Statistics show that if a person doesn't get sent back to prison within five years of being released, their chances of never going back are good. My dream is to establish an apartment complex where residents can live in a drug and alcohol-free environment and have a support system. They'll be on their own, paying their own rent and bills, coming and going as they please. Only they won't have constant tempta-tion around them. At least not in the place where they live."

"I like that dream," I said. "Wish it could come true in time for me to live there."

She smiled at me—a kind of half-smile. "I wish it could, too."

I stood to leave a second time. Regina caught one of my hands in both of hers and looked up at me.

"Never go back, Gracene," she said, like she was pleading with me.

"Go back?"

"To Egypt."

CHAPTER FIFTEEN

mull—*to study or ruminate; ponder; to think about carefully*
conjure—*to produce or bring about by or as if by magic*
sadistic—*deriving pleasure from extreme cruelty*
devastate—*to lay waste or render desolate; to overwhelm*

I SAT ON THE COUCH AND ATE A DINNER MADE UP OF LAST NIGHT'S leftovers. The only light in the room came from the twinkling bulbs on our tree. Thanks to the conversation with Regina, I was mulling over this fool's mission I was on with Del. A knock on the door brought my meal and the mulling to an end.

I opened it, and there stood Del. In the glare of the porch light, he looked like a demon I'd conjured up just by thinking about him. Like before, he didn't wait for an invitation to come in. He barged past me and took a seat on the couch. His eyes darted around the room and finally came to rest on our tree.

"Well, look at that," he said, "a Christmas tree." He was jitterier than ever and scratched his arms like he had a rash—or fleas. "That's real nice. And good timing, too, 'cause I got a little present for you. Some information you're gonna like."

"Oh yeah?" I had serious doubts about that and didn't even try to hide it.

"My friend Sid has located Shirley."

I kept calm on the outside, but my insides were wound to the point of snapping. "That so? Where'd he find her?" It was all I could do to keep my voice steady.

"You know how I told you Sid heard she was working in a coffee shop? Well, turns out that wasn't Shirley after all. But crazy thing, that woman knew Shirley and gave Sid some information. He followed her lead and danged if he didn't find your mama." He leaned toward me, resting his elbows on his bouncing knees. "But it weren't easy."

"What do you mean?"

"She's changed her name, first and last. Made it mighty hard to find her."

"So what's her name now?"

He let out a sigh through fluttering lips. " 'Fraid I can't tell you that."

"Why not?"

"'Cause I don't know it. Sid's a friend, but he can also be a real jerk sometimes. He's holding on to that information 'til I give him more money. Guess you could say he's holding it for ransom."

I swore under my breath. This didn't surprise me. I was ninety-nine percent sure this whole scheme was pure bull, something Del had cooked up to get money out of me. And the shape he was in made it loud and clear he needed that money to buy more of whatever he was on. I was close to throwing him out on his ear, but ... there was that other one percent.

"How much money you talking about, Del? And believe me when I say I don't have a spare dime to my name."

"I know, I know," he said. "But I might have a solution for that."

I ignored all the alarms going off inside me. "What kind of solution?"

He sniffed—something he'd been doing a lot of. "I'm not much of a believer in fate," he said, "but sometimes I do think things were just meant to be. I met a guy named Dennis in a bar one night, and we got to be pretty good buddies. Come to find out, he knows you. Says he'd worked with you at a landscaping business before he got laid off. That right?" He must've taken my silence as a yes. He wiped his nose on his shirt sleeve and continued talking. "We got together again a few days ago. He says he heard you were working at the business's storage barn now with a guy named Tony. Same guy who laid him off." His eyebrows went up like he wanted me to confirm that information.

"So what's your point?"

"Dennis told me he knew for a fact there was a lot of expensive equipment stored in that barn and—"

"You can stop right there, Del." My pulse throbbed against my eardrums with loud *whooshes*. "I don't like where this conversation is headed. Time for you to go." I pushed myself out of the recliner and walked to the door.

"Now hold on, Gracene," he said. "Hear me out. Dennis and me have a plan for starting a lawn care business. Of course, no one is going to bankroll an ex-con or a guy outta work, but I know someone who'll fork out good money for the kind of tools and equipment that's in that barn."

"I'm not listening to this," I said. "Even if I wanted to take a chance on spending the rest of my life in prison, no way I'm going to steal from Richard or betray Tony. Those guys gave me a break when no one else would. And they *trust* me. But I guess you wouldn't have any idea what that means."

Del rubbed his hands over his face. "*Pssshh*. You don't understand, Gracene." He spoke like I was some kind of moron for not jumping at this chance. "We're not asking you to do the actual stealing. Me and Dennis will take all the risks. We just need a little assistance. No one will ever know you were involved." Now he was shaking bad and clawing at his arms. "Dennis has been out to that barn with Tony to pick up supplies. He knows there's a lock that opens with a code. We just need that code."

"No, Del." I shook my head hard. "Not gonna happen."

His voice got higher, and he spoke fast. "Now, look, Gracene, you're not thinking straight. You're not taking any chance at all, yet me and Dennis are willing to give you a piece of the take. Enough for you to find out Shirley's new name. And as far as hurting your employer, he's got all that equipment insured. Hell, he'll be better off. Get to replace it with brand new stuff."

I couldn't count the number of times I'd heard arguments like that. There'd always been the sure-fire plan, the risk-free scheme, the nobody-gets-hurt scam. That kind of talk had cost me six years of my life. I jerked open the door and pointed into the dark. "Get. Out."

He made no motion to leave. Instead, he leaned against the back of the couch, like he was settling in. "Well, that's not very neighborly of you, Gracene, but I don't take no offense. In fact, I'm gonna give you something. I'm gonna tell you what I did learn about your mama."

I should've run out that door myself, but news about Mama was to me what hooch is to a wino. I crossed my arms over my chest and listened.

Del curled his lips into a cruel smile, like he was getting some sort of sadistic pleasure from what he was about to say. "Seems ol' Shirley found herself a rich husband. Living in a fancy house in a swanky part of town with him and his teenage daughter." He barked out a laugh. "Who would've ever thought it? Fireball Shirley Hollowell a regular June Cleaver."

Rage and shock drained the blood supply from my brain. I leaned against the door frame behind me to keep from crumbling to the floor. Memories of all those years of hurting and feeling worthless flooded my head. I remembered the times I'd been lonely and scared and hungry and broke. The terrifying nights in jail cells that smelled like pee and vomit. The days on end without a decent meal. Most of all, I remembered all those experiences leading to the most devastating decision of my life.

At times I'd wondered if Mama was even alive. Now I find out not only she was alive, but she'd been living a life of luxury and hadn't given me a second thought. She hadn't just deserted me, she'd thrown me over for a new life. And a new daughter. I wondered if the new daughter was cute and little.

I blinked back hot tears. When I could squeeze the words past the lump in my throat, I spoke. "Let me think about it."

Del walked to the door and stood right next to me. "Okay, you think about it," he said in a way that sounded more like a threat than a suggestion. "But I'd think real hard if I was you. I'd think about that so-called mama of yours, sittin' in her fancy house with her brand new family and not even caring if you're alive. I'd think about finding her and letting her know what misery and *danger*"—he came down heavy on that word—"she'd put me through." His chuckle was more of a growl. "Who knows? She might give you some money to shut you up. To make sure you don't come around and mess up her cushy life."

He pressed against me, trapping me between him and the door frame. I was sure he could feel my heart pounding. I didn't know if it was fear or hate that kept me frozen in place.

"You think about it," he said. "I'll be back to get your answer. That's a promise."

He stepped through the door and then turned back to me. "Oh, I almost forgot," he said with a sneer. "Merry Christmas."

~

I dropped into the recliner, panting and sweating like I'd just churned up fifty acres with a lawn tiller. I had to hand it to Del.

He might be a BB brain about most things, but when it came to me, he was pure genius. He figured the information he gave me would turn my longing to find Mama into a passion for revenge. And, God help me, he was right.

God help me. I don't know why, but when those words popped into my head, my eyes went to the nativity scene under the tree. It was such a far-fetched story—that a loving, all-powerful God would come to earth as a helpless baby and then die so people like me could be forgiven. And yet, I'd wanted to believe it. I'd wanted to convince myself it was true.

I found enough energy to make my way to my bedroom and climb into bed. I don't know how long I'd been there when I heard the click-clack of the chime. Hallie was home.

The outside temperature was just above freezing. Inside Tony's pickup, where I was about to break a sweat, he hummed some song I didn't recognize. He hummed pretty loud, but not loud enough to drown out the voice in my head. The voice that told me no one would ever connect me with the crime and I was a fool not to go along with Del's scheme. The voice that yelled Mama deserved to hear how she'd wrecked my life.

Over the racket in my brain, I heard Tony speak. "You got any plans for Christmas Day, Gracene?"

"Not really." I huddled against the passenger door, as far away from him as possible.

"Why don't you join me and my family for lunch?"

Whoa. Hadn't seen that coming. From his stories, I knew Tony's family was a loud and fun bunch. Also, Hallie had been spending a lot of her spare time with Sean, so I figured I'd be alone most of Christmas Day, holed up in the apartment. I wanted to take him up on his offer, but I couldn't. I was still deciding whether or not to take Del up on his.

"Better not," I mumbled. "Wouldn't want to put y'all out."

"Nonsense. You know how many relatives I have. And you know how much we like food. One more person won't make a dent."

"Yeah, well, okay." I tried to ignore the guilt nibbling at my insides.

Tony stopped the truck outside the equipment barn, and we both got out. At the door, I positioned myself so I could see the code Tony punched in. It was an easy matter of moving about two inches to the right of where I usually stood. He didn't notice a thing. And even if he had, it wouldn't have made any difference. He trusted me that much. If guilt had been nibbling at me before, now it was gnawing like a nasty rat.

I couldn't keep my mind on my work the rest of that day. I'd never been so miserable—even in prison. Always before, the rotten things I'd done could be blamed on the people who'd wronged me, starting with Mama. Now I didn't have that excuse. Now there were people in my corner. People who cared about me, helped me, *trusted* me. And I was about to stick it to all of them.

I avoided Tony as much as I could. It wasn't easy since there were only four people working in the warehouse. He must've noticed something was wrong but didn't say anything.

As I replaced worn out rake handles, all I could think about was how Tony had put himself on the line for me—maybe even risked his own job. Then Regina and how much she believed in me came to mind. And Hallie? She would've locked me in my bedroom before letting me go through with this.

All afternoon I tried to push the guilt to the back of my mind. It would go there for a while but wouldn't stay. Then I tried some wishful thinking. Maybe Del would hightail it out of town or get himself arrested again.

During my break, I went into the office and brewed another

pot of coffee. I didn't have to worry about the caffeine keeping me awake. I had too much on my mind to sleep.

~

"There they are, Gracene." Regina pointed to five dusty boxes stacked in the corner of the community room. They were stuffed to overflowing with fake greenery, tinsel, and tangled strings of Christmas lights. She headed toward her office. "Go through them and use what you need."

Strange choice of words, I thought. I didn't *need* any of that junk. What I needed was to be back in my bed, catching up on the sleep I'd lost the past few days. I needed a hot breakfast and strong coffee and some peace of mind. Instead, I was up at the crack of dawn on a Saturday, barely surviving on a bowl of corn flakes and wrestling with nerves as jumbled as those decorations.

I sat in the middle of the community room floor and began working out the snarls in miles and miles of lights. I didn't hold back my cussing, although—with Regina right next door in her office—I did keep it low. Two hours later, I'd undone the last knot in the last string. I was coiling it around my arm when I heard a motorcycle pull into the parking lot. Even through the walls, I recognized the unmistakable roar of a Harley.

Seconds later, Chase stepped through the door, dressed in insulated coveralls and a stocking cap. "Kenneth said he thought you'd be putting up lights today. Said you might could use some help."

It took every ounce of my self-control not to run across the room and kiss him right on the lips. Instead, I held out a coil of lights. "A job this size requires a *few* good men." I gave him a smile and a wink. "But I'll settle for one."

Me and Chase worked solid for the next three hours. We made a good team and managed to get the downstairs done in record time. Being busy and breathing the fresh air helped me forget my troubles for a while.

The morning had grown warmer, and Chase stopped to take off his coveralls and cap. "I've worked up an appetite. How about you?"

"Starving." My cereal had given out an hour ago. I figured I should offer Chase some lunch since he'd helped me all morning, but the only thing I had in the apartment was peanut butter, bread, and canned soup. Somehow, I didn't think he'd be interested in that. I didn't have two quarters to rub together, so I couldn't buy him anything, either.

"How about a hamburger?" he asked. "My treat."

"Sounds good to me."

We walked a couple of blocks to a hamburger joint. On opposite sides of a booth, we spread out our food on the table: two huge cheeseburgers, two large orders of fries, and two super-sized coffees. I'd become more comfortable around him, and we talked as we ate. We started out discussing our jobs, and that flowed naturally into a conversation about his work at Resurrection Church.

"It's an old building," he said. "Something is always breaking down, and funds are always tight. I do what I can in my spare time. It keeps me hopping."

"I'll bet. It's got to be frustrating, too. Why do you do it? I mean, I wonder why working around a bunch of prisoners and ex-prisoners would interest you. From what you said at Thanksgiving, I know you never spent any time inside."

Chase didn't seem to mind my nosiness. "No, I didn't," he said. "But only by the grace of God." He ate the last bite of his burger and wiped his mouth with a napkin. "My mom was divorced and raised me and my two little brothers by herself. She worked two jobs, so she expected my brothers and me to pull our weight. And we paid for it if we didn't." He chuckled. "My drill sergeant in the Marines could've taken lessons from her."

"So you didn't exactly have a *Brady Bunch* childhood, either."

He ran his hand over his short hair, which—I noticed for the first time—had a few streaks of gray. "Not even close," he said. "I'll hand it to my mom, she tried. But she couldn't watch us round the clock, and we lived in a rough neighborhood. I got in with a bad crowd and had some close calls with the law. Fortunately, I wised up before I got into serious trouble and decided the best way for me to have any kind of future was to join the service."

"And that's how you got your degree."

"Yeah, I got my education paid for. But I got a lot more. In Afghanistan there was a sergeant who was a Christian. We became friends, and because of him, I became a Christian, too." Chase clasped his hands on the table and studied them. "One day my squad was part of a convoy that came under attack by a small group of Taliban fighters. My friend led our team to go after them. When we located them, we managed to take out most of the pack, but a few scattered. The sergeant covered our withdrawal, and our team made it back to the convoy safely." Chase cleared his throat, and there was a catch in his voice as he spoke his next sentence. "Everyone but the sergeant."

"Man, that's tough. I'm so sorry." Without thinking, I laid my hand on his forearm.

He sat up straighter in the booth but didn't move his arm. "No, I'm sorry. I didn't mean to bring up old war stories. But you asked why I volunteer at Resurrection Church. I work there because I want to do something to honor my friend. Something that would show my life has been worth his sacrifice."

He flattened his palms on the table and spread out his fingers. "I like to work with my hands, and I like figuring out how to fix things. Resurrection Church gives me lots of opportunities for that."

His fingers were thick and stubby. There were scrapes on his knuckles and traces of grease around his nails. I didn't understand how hands could look so strong and gentle at the same time, and it was all I could do not to reach out and take them in mine.

We sat for a few moments without speaking. Then he gathered up our trash. "Time's a-wastin'," he said, sliding out of the booth. "If we want to finish those decorations before sunset, we'd better get to it."

We walked back to Transformation Place and worked the rest of the afternoon on the second story. We put lights and garland along every inch of the overhang and wound them around the railing as well. Just as daylight was fading and the cold was settling in again, we stood by an electrical outlet.

"Now for the moment of truth," Chase said. He grabbed the end of the light string and knelt. With a sweep of his arm, he made a big show of inserting the plug into the outlet. I laughed, but my heart was in my throat. I was dead tired. If those lights didn't come on, I was seriously going to fling myself over the rail.

Luckily, I didn't have to. When the connection was made, the lights came on with a burst of color. They twinkled all around the courtyard.

I let out a whoop, and Chase pumped his fist in the air. "Booyah!" he yelled. Then he grabbed me in a bear hug and swung me around like I was as light as a ballerina.

After we cleaned up the decorating mess, I stood on the second-floor walkway and watched him charge from the parking lot on his Harley. For the first time in years, I let myself dream—of a normal life with a husband and kids. Of belonging to an honest-to-goodness family.

CHAPTER SIXTEEN

sheepish—*embarrassed or bashful, as by having done something wrong or foolish*
comprehension—*perception or understanding*

REGINA STOOD AT THE FRONT OF THE CROWDED COMMUNITY ROOM and barked out orders. "Okay, don't anyone open your gifts until they've all been distributed!"

I huddled in a corner at the very back and tried to make myself invisible. I would've skipped this circus altogether, but Regina had insisted all residents attend.

She'd worked hard on the Christmas party, making sure there was plenty of food and presents for all the residents and their children. Still, my plan was to listen for my name, claim my gift, and make a fast getaway.

I spotted Chase at the refreshment table. When he smiled and nodded at me, I scooted further down in my chair. I didn't want to feed ridiculous dreams of a romance between us, so I'd been avoiding him the past couple of weeks at church.

He walked to my corner and pulled up a folding chair. "Want one?" He held out a handful of snickerdoodles.

I shook my head.

He shrugged and shoved an entire cookie into his mouth. "Complete bedlam," he said as he chewed and looked around the room, but his lopsided grin told me he was enjoying himself.

"You have kids?" he asked.

"Nope."

"Me, neither. Have plans for Christmas Day?" He was certainly getting chatty.

"Yeah. Planning to go to a friend's house." That wasn't a lie exactly. I did have plans. Just had no intention of keeping them. "What about you? Are you spending it with your mom and brothers?"

"Mom died two years ago," he said. He offered me another cookie, and this time I took it. "But tomorrow I'll have dinner with my middle brother and his family."

I took a bite and brushed cookie crumbs from my shirt. "What about your youngest brother?"

Chase pressed his lips into a line. "Cory," he said. "He's in prison in Kansas. I guess he's another reason I help out at Resurrection Church."

That news caught me off guard but also slightly eased my mind. It was a little something me and Chase had in common. "Makes sense," I said. "You help out here, and maybe someone in Kansas helps you by helping your brother. Not exactly karma, but kind of like it."

He leaned back in his chair and rested a foot on the opposite knee. "Oh, I'm not a big fan of karma, Gracene. That suggests we get what we deserve." He gave me the most relaxed smile I'd ever seen from him—one that made my heart do a little leap. "These days, I'm more into grace."

～

On Christmas Eve residents who weren't visiting friends or relatives attended the candlelight service at Resurrection Church. With all the guilt weighing on me, I dreaded going, but it was required.

Even though I'd never attended church on Christmas Eve, I knew what to expect from TV shows and stories. Lighted candles, Christmas carols, and a pageant of shepherds and wise men were a far cry from the boozing, brawling celebrations I'd grown up with. I guarded my emotions by resuming my old habit of zoning out. I sat through the entire service stone-faced and frozen in the pew. Meanwhile, Hallie sat beside me, her face glowing like she'd just met the Holy Family in person.

Back in our apartment after church, her holiday spirit continued to bubble over. She'd invited her Bible study group to our apartment for a "little Christmas Eve snack," and had conned me into helping. I was arranging thumbprint cookies—another of Flo's recipes—on a tray, when Hallie came up to me, holding one hand behind her back.

"I want to give you this before everyone arrives," she said. She brought her hand in front of her and held out a gift.

When I unwrapped it, I found a Bible with my name printed on it in gold letters.

"I didn't know if you'd want a Bible," Hallie said in a sheepish voice. "But the other day I saw an old one on your bureau, so I thought ... maybe ..."

The Bible she'd seen had been laying around in the community room for a long time with no one claiming it. One day, out of the blue, Regina said I was welcomed to it if I wanted it. I'm not sure why I took the worn out thing—considering I was a lost cause and all—but I did. I'd never opened it, much less read it.

I lifted this new Bible to my nose and breathed in the smell of the leather cover. "It's beautiful, Hallie. Thank you."

The Bible must've cost a lot of money. I thought about the cash I'd given Del and the cheap fuzzy socks I'd bought for her and decided to give them to her later.

"I'm so pleased you like it," she said, smiling from ear to ear. She took the Bible from me and opened it. "Look. There are notes at the bottom of each page. In case you don't understand what you read."

The new pages with gold edges crackled as she turned to the back. "And this section? It's the concordance. Let's say you need ... uhm ..."—she ran her index finger down the page and came to a stop—"forgiveness. See. Just look at all these scriptures about it." She flipped to a page and read. "1 John 1:9. If we confess our sins, he is faithful and just and will forgive us ..." She handed the Bible back to me. "See how easy it is?"

I didn't know if she was talking about the concordance or if this was another pitch for becoming a Christian. I thanked her for the new Bible again, although I doubted it would get any more use than the old one.

～

The Christmas Days I'd spent in prison were downright jolly compared to the one I went through at Transformation Place. Hallie begged me to join her and Sean and their Bible study group for a pot luck lunch in his apartment. I turned her down. I also backed out of Tony's invitation to spend Christmas afternoon with his family. Knowing what I was about to do to him, I would've never made it through the day without a meltdown.

In the three weeks since Del had shown up at my apartment with his "proposal," guilt had all but hamstrung me. At times it would become so crushing I'd decide I wouldn't give him the code. Then I'd remember how much I wanted to find Mama. And then how his last words to me had sounded like a threat.

The long empty day stretched into an eternity. I was bone tired but couldn't sleep. At one point, I grew so desperate I got my new Bible from my room. I sat in my recliner and thumbed through it, but even with the study notes, my scrambled mind couldn't make sense of anything I read. I laid it on the lamp table beside the chair and paced around the apartment until I ran out of energy. Then I collapsed on my bed and cried myself to sleep.

~

Three days after Christmas—just when I dared to hope Del really had disappeared—he knocked on my door. He looked even skinnier than he did four weeks ago. His hair was thinner and greasier, and you could've sunk a golf ball in the hollow spaces under his cheekbones. He smelled like ammonia, a sure sign he was on meth.

"You got a belated Christmas present for me, Gracene?" he asked.

"Let me get it."

The sooner this deal was over, the better. I left him standing in the doorway and stepped over to the lamp table. With my back to the door, I leaned down and took the paper with the code written on it from the drawer. My heart was slamming against my ribs. So much was riding on this tiny slip of paper. It could lead to Mama. And it could possibly save my life.

As I straightened my back, I saw it—the Bible I'd left on the table Christmas Day. I stared at it, unable to move my eyes away or even blink. Faces flashed across the cover—Hallie's ... Regina's ... Tony's ... Chase's. My conscience kicked in with the force of a lightning bolt, and I leaned on top of the recliner to catch my breath. The faces reminded me that for the first time in a long, long time, people cared about me. And I cared about them. *Was I really going to do this?*

I was still staring at the Bible when another face appeared: Mama's. She was smiling the same smile as in my photo. If I found her, I could finally solve the mystery behind that smile. I could ask the question that had hounded me every day of my life for twenty-two years: *Why did you leave me?* The paper in my hand probably held the last chance of ever getting the answer, but it wasn't worth betraying people I loved.

Leaning on the chair and trembling, I choked out the words, "Bye-bye, Mama. Have a good life ... wherever you are." I reached for her, but her face and smile grew fainter until they were completely gone.

I managed to get my breathing and shaking under control and walked back to the door. "Sorry, Del." I curled my fingers tight around the paper. "Guess I lost that code. Got nothing for you." I shoved on the door, but before it closed, he stuck his foot between it and the frame.

"Hey, don't be unfriendly," he said through the slit. "I got a present for you. Information about your mama."

I kicked at his steel-toed work boot, but it wouldn't budge. "I don't believe you," I said. "You haven't got a thing. Probably never did. All this was just a sick plan of yours to weasel money out of me." I continued kicking at his foot and pushing hard against the door.

"That ain't true!" he yelled and pushed back. "And I know you got that code. Give it to me."

For a skinny, whacked-out druggie, Del was strong. I strained and grunted and pressed as hard as I could. When I felt my strength giving out, I looked into his face for some sign he was growing tired, too.

The Christmas lights strung around the building blinked on and off and made the sliver of Del's face blood-red one second and black as a demon's the next. The hate streaming from it burned my skin.

The night was crisp and cold and still. But out of nowhere a breeze stirred, and the tinkling of a wind chime came from the apartment down the way. I hadn't noticed the sound in months, but that night, over the noise of Del's dog-like panting and my own heavy breathing, it was clear as a bell. Clear as the wind chime I'd heard in my nightmare.

Pictures whirled in my mind, fuzzy at first but growing sharper. There was an old, wooden shed, filled with cobwebs. I was five years old, and a man had locked me inside. I crouched in the corner, covering my head and crying. Then I lifted my face and watched in terror as a spider crawled across the webs. Like a mechanical monster, it lifted and lowered spindly legs and made slow and steady progress toward a moth that fought to free itself. I released wails of fear and rage.

The man's voice came through slits in the shed's walls. "Ain't doin' you no good to yell, Gracene. No one's around 'cept me." I howled like a trapped animal and covered my head again.

With another tinkling of the chime, the shed disappeared, and a dark wood replaced it. Tangled vines and branches clawed at my skin. A man had me slung over his shoulder, and I was pounding my fists against his back. He'd tied a rope around my waist and was heading in the direction of the pond on Aunt Shannon's place. "There's 'gators in that pond, Gracene, and I'm gonna catch me one," the man said. "You're my bait." I couldn't see his face, but I recognized the voice. It was the same one that had come from outside the shed.

I felt myself being hoisted into the air, and the next second I was running. Running through the woods. Running like the devil himself was chasing me.

When I heard the voice again, it came from inches away.

"I know you got that code," Del was saying in a raspy voice. "You always was a lousy little liar." He laughed—low and mean.

Shock set my head reeling and caused me to let up on my pushing. The door flew open, and I was staring straight into Del's face. "It was you," I said.

He returned my stare through the eyes of a corpse. Flat, vacant, unseeing eyes. Eyes saturated by a black so heavy and endless that not even the slightest spark of life could pierce it. Then he blinked, and fury replaced the darkness.

In a heartbeat, he lunged through the doorway and grabbed

my shoulders. The few seconds it took him to kick the door shut and shove me across the living room seemed to drag on for hours. I opened my mouth to scream, but nothing came out.

He pinned me against a wall, and his fingers dug into my skin. "You don't know what you're talkin' about, Gracene! You don't know *nothin'*, you hear?" His words were slow and drawn out, and they rang in my ears like they came from the bottom of a pit. "You got that code! Give it to me!"

He pressed his left forearm across my neck. I tugged at it, while he pushed his right hand into my pockets and underneath my clothes. His cold, scaly hand made my skin crawl. He worked it down my arm to my clenched fist.

"Well, well, what we got here?" he crooned as he pried at my fingers.

I opened my mouth again. This time gurgling came out.

"Shut up!" He let go of my fist and clamped his hand over my nose and mouth. "Think you're too good to help me out, don't ya'? You're mama thought she was better 'n me, too. Well, I showed her, didn't I? Terrorized her little girl. Her precious little Gracene."

He moved his hand off my face and his forearm off my neck, and in that split-second, I gasped for air. Then, like a snake coiling around my neck, his hands clamped around my throat. He shouted, "You don't know nothin', ya' hear?" He continued to press me against the wall, while over and over, he screamed, "Ya' hear me?"

I couldn't swallow or breathe, and my lungs were on fire. My head was a volcano about to erupt. I clutched Del's wrists and tried to pull them apart, but they wouldn't budge. My legs were growing weak, and I could feel myself sliding to the floor. What little light was in the room began to fade, and then ... total darkness.

Click. Clack. Click-clack, click-clack. The sound forced its way through the inky sludge in my head—confusing at first and then unmistakable. It came from outside the door and a voice—a high, squeaky one —said, "Hold on, Gracene. Help is coming."

When I heard those words, hope shot through me like an adrenaline fix, and from deep inside me came another message: *You've been a fighter all your life. This is no time to quit.*

The hope turned to white-hot rage.

~

I woke up in a hospital room with the sun shining through open blinds. My mouth felt like a pillow had been stuffed in it, and my left eye was swollen almost shut. Every little move caused me to wince. I'd been in plenty of fights in my lifetime. Nothing had ever hurt like this.

"Morning, Gracene. Welcome back to the land of the living."

Even though I was groggy, I recognized Regina's voice. A neck brace kept me from turning toward her.

She stood close to my bed and whispered. "Do you remember how you got here?"

Bits and pieces of the previous night began breaking through the fog in my mind. Every word I spoke rubbed against my raw throat like sandpaper, but—drifting in and out of la-la land—I confessed to Regina why I had the code to the warehouse. I described how Del attacked me when I wouldn't give him the code and how I thought my life was over. "Hallie tapped the chime ... help on the way. Started fighting."

Somehow Regina managed to connect the dots. "You fought, alright. From what I understand, when the police caught up with Del, his face looked like he'd tangled with a wildcat. And lost." She gave a low chuckle. "And good job with that knee-to-groin move. They say it might be a while before he can stand up straight."

I ran my tongue over my tender, swollen lips. "Don't

remember much. Shouting, Sean's face ... lots of people in my apartment."

Regina scooted a chair next to the bed and settled into it. "Hallie got home from work last night and heard shouts and threats coming from inside the apartment. She heard a man's raspy voice and recognized it right away as Del's. Her first thought was to charge in and rescue you but then she remembered the last time she saw Del he'd had a gun. So she ran to the first place she thought of—Sean's apartment."

Regina closed her eyes. "I hope I've got all this straight. Sean heard banging on his door and answered it. The instant he saw Hallie's face and heard her say 'Gracene,' he grabbed a dumbbell—the closest thing he had to a weapon—and rushed to your apartment. Hallie tried to warn him about the gun, but he was already gone. She called 911 and then called me. Thankfully, your door wasn't locked, and Sean was able to burst right in." Regina slid forward in the chair and grasped the edge of the mattress. "He saw you and Del rolling on the floor, and Del had his hands around your throat. Sean screamed at him to let you go, and I guess Del realized he was no match for a strong young man armed with a dumbbell. He managed to get to his feet and run out the door. Sean didn't try to stop him or go after him. His main concern was checking on you." Regina let out a long breath. "If Sean hadn't arrived when he did, I hate to think what would've happened. The police were there in a matter of minutes, and the ambulance was right on their tail."

Pain shot through my neck and shoulders, and I moaned.

Regina stood and gently rubbed my hand, careful of the scrapes and bruises. "Take it easy. You're going to be sore for a while, but the doctors say you have no permanent injuries. Not physical ones, anyway. They want to keep you here a day or two for observation. Just to be sure."

I was so tired. But I wouldn't rest easy until I knew. "Del?"

"Right where he belongs. The police caught him about a half

block from the apartment. Said he was in too bad of shape to get far. He's in custody now. If he survives prison, by the time he gets out he'll be wearing diapers and taking his nourishment through a straw. Too old and feeble to cause any more trouble."

I closed my eyes, but sleep didn't come for a long time.

CHAPTER SEVENTEEN

sear—*to burn or char the surface of; to brand*
carcass—*the dead body of an animal; anything from which life and power are gone*

THE NEXT MORNING I WASN'T AS STIFF, AND MY THROAT FELT better. But my wounds were still tender. I managed to turn my head enough to see someone had left an African violet on my bedside table. I could barely make out the scratchy handwriting on the card: *Semper fi, Chase.*

My first visitors were the police. They asked a lot of questions, and for the first time in my life, I was glad to cooperate with them. They told me when they saw Del's bloodied face and hands, they almost felt sorry for him. Almost.

Other visitors came that morning—residents from Transformation Place and members of Resurrection Church. I teared up every time someone entered my room. Kenneth stopped by, and after him, Tony. Tony told me not to come back to work until I was sure I was okay. "And don't worry about your pay. Richard has you covered." At that point, the waterworks came on full force.

Between visitors I tried to rest, but my mind wouldn't let me. At last I knew who the child in my dream was and who had been the creeper outside the window. But I couldn't figure out who'd done the screaming. Or maybe I just didn't want to. Other disturbing thoughts kept me awake, too.

Late afternoon, Hallie came in carrying a brown sack and the Bible she'd given me. The minute we saw each other, we started blubbering. But I was still too sore for a hug.

She placed the sack on my bedside table. "This is from Flo. When I told her what happened to you, she made some chicken soup from her great-grandmother's recipe. Said when your throat doesn't hurt anymore, she'll make you some bread pudding." Hallie smiled hesitantly as she laid the Bible beside the sack. "And I thought you might like to have this."

She pulled a chair close to my bed and sat on the edge of it. "I wanted to come yesterday, but Regina told me to wait and let you get some rest. I was so worried about you, Gracene. I stayed up all night praying you'd be okay." Dark circles under her eyes told me she wasn't exaggerating. She kind of slumped in the chair, but after a few seconds, she perked up. "With Flo's soup and my prayers, you'll recover in no time!"

"Tell Flo thanks for the soup." I croaked out the words like a bullfrog. "And thank you for saving my life."

She ducked her chin. "I didn't do anything but run for help. Sean's the hero."

I picked up on the pride in her voice and grinned. I noticed she hadn't called my rescue a miracle. Sean got all the credit.

She stood and straightened her sweater. "I better go and let you get some rest. I can't wait until you're out of here. Even if you're not much of a talker, I miss your company." She tilted her head. "Makes me wonder what I'll do when you move out for good."

My stomach lurched when she said that. I'd been wondering the same thing about myself.

Her mouth formed a tight smile. "Oh, well. I'll worry about that when the time comes." She turned and walked to the door.

As she pulled on the handle, my words escaped in a kind of wail. "Wait, Hallie. Don't go yet."

She rushed back to my bed and reached for the call button. "Should I call a nurse? Are you in pain?"

"No, I'm not in pain. At least, not in my body."

She wrinkled her forehead. "Where then?"

"In my soul."

"Want to talk?" she asked softly and sat back down.

I did want to talk, but finding the right words was hard. "Laying in this bed has given me time to do a lot of thinking," I said finally. "I've thought about the people who've been so good to me. Regina, you, Sean. I can't wrap my mind around the idea that volunteers—people who don't even know me—have worked so hard to give me a place to live and help me get on my feet. Kenneth and Tony and Chase and the residents ..." I gave my head a careful shake. "I can't begin to name them all and the good things they've done for me."

"So why does that cause you pain?"

"I see those people's faces so full of love and goodness and light. And then I see Del's." I bit my lip to keep it from quivering.

Hallie stood and placed her hand on my shoulder. "You don't need to be afraid of Del anymore. He'll never hurt you again." She took a tissue from her jeans pocket and dabbed very gently at my tears.

"It's not that." I squeezed my eyes shut and immediately opened them. The hideous image had been there again. Like it was seared to the backs of my eyelids. "Every time I shut my eyes, I see Del's face. Not a human face at all but a skull. And the sockets are bottomless, black pits. At first I thought it was evil that made his eyes that way, but now I know it's something worse. It's emptiness." I shuddered. "There's *nothing* there. Like the last drop of anything that ever made him human has been squeezed out. Like God himself has given up on him."

I pulled the blanket to my chin and gripped it tight. "I'm so afraid," I said, shivering. "I don't want to end up like Del. I don't want God to give up on me."

Hallie shook her head. "Gracene, God doesn't abandon people. They abandon him. You've heard my story. He is always willing—he *longs*—to forgive us."

"I wish I could believe that. But you don't know what I did." I covered my face with my hands, and sobs shook my body. "How can I ask for God's forgiveness me, when I can't even forgive myself?"

"You don't have to forgive yourself," she said softly. "In fact, you probably can't. But that doesn't mean God won't forgive you. You might have to live with remorse over what you did, but—"

"I had an abortion."

At last I'd said it. Or more like spit it out—the hated word that had gnawed at my gut for eight years like maggots feasting on road kill. It bounced off the walls like the bang of a judge's gavel and then hung heavy in the air.

I lowered my hands and sucked in a deep breath. "I was twenty—"

"You know you don't have to explain to me," Hallie said.

But I knew I did. If I kept this secret hidden any longer, it would destroy me.

"I was twenty years old," I repeated. "Things were going good for me. Between a job at a convenience store and extra cash coming from a check-forging scheme, I was making enough money to rent a little apartment and buy groceries and booze. Sheldon was living with me. He wasn't really my boyfriend, but I liked him okay. And he helped with the rent.

"One weekend me and him partied a little too hard, and, well, one thing led to another. A few weeks later, I was peeing on a stick and staring at a plus sign."

I looked over at Hallie. When I didn't see shock or disgust on her face, I continued. "I was scared, but once I got over my panic, a part of me was happy. For the first time since Mama left, there'd be someone for me to love and someone who'd love me. I'd finally have the chance of being part of a normal family. I never would've deliberately conceived a child to fulfill a selfish dream like that, but"—I shrugged—"since it happened."

"What about Sheldon?" Hallie asked. "How did he feel about it?"

"Sheldon had his faults, but he wasn't a complete loser—or so I thought. I convinced myself we could make a go of marriage. But when I told him about the baby, practically the first word out of his mouth was *abortion*. Said he'd help pay for it." I gave a bitter laugh. "Quite the gentlemen, huh?"

I couldn't tell if Hallie's head shake was an answer to my question or one of disbelief.

"We argued," I said, "but in the end, Sheldon won. The kicker is he convinced me to do it by promising I could still have that family I'd always wanted. He said he loved me. Said that when we got our lives together and saved a little money, we'd get married and have lots of kids. And we could give them the things we'd never be able to give this child."

I swallowed to relieve the aching in my throat. "After a few agonizing days of deciding what to do, I went through with the abortion. And guess what? A week after that, I came home from work and found Sheldon had cleared out. Had vanished without leaving behind so much as a sock. I haven't seen or heard from him since." Tears stung the scratches on my face. "I believed the words of a worthless liar and ended the life of an innocent child."

I turned my head away from Hallie. She'd met every confession I'd made about my past with understanding. Sometimes even laughter. But I was afraid this was one of my sins she couldn't excuse or overlook. If her innocent part in an accidental death had caused her so much grief, the idea of someone deliberately taking a tiny, helpless life would horrify her.

For a long while, muted footsteps and calls of people in the hallway were the only sounds in the room. Then I heard Hallie stirring and figured she was leaving. But instead of the opening and closing of the door, there was the rustling of pages. Hallie began reading in a confident voice.

"'For God so loved everyone that he gave his one and only Son, that whoever believes in him shall not perish but have eternal life.' You see," she said, "God lost a child, too. He knows your anguish, your pain, your sense of loss because he experienced the same thing."

I turned my head toward her. "But God doesn't know my guilt. He sacrificed his child to save the world. I sacrificed mine to save myself."

"I'm going to read this verse again," Hallie said. "Listen very carefully."

I don't know if she deliberately emphasized *whoever* and *everyone* the second time she read the verse or if I heard it that way because I was so desperate to believe it. Whichever it was, I let those words sink in. Then, with the joy and relief that comes with a not-guilty verdict, I realized *whoever* and *everyone* included me. No matter what I'd done, God's gift of Jesus had provided a way of forgiveness. All I had to do was accept it.

With Hallie's help, I prayed. I'm not sure I understood everything I was saying, but I did understand this: For the first time since Mama left, I didn't feel abandoned, and the weight of thinking I was a hopeless loser had lifted from my heart. I was forgiven.

There hadn't been goose bumps, no rush of wind, no voice either inner or outer. But a sense of peace I'd never known settled over me like a warm blanket, and I slept.

~

I'd been back at Transformation Place and on the mend for three days when I got another summons. Not from Regina and not from the state—from Aunt Shannon. At first, I refused to answer her phone calls. But she kept on until I caved.

Regina drove me out to her place and waited for me in the van. I didn't have any warm fuzzies about this family reunion, but I wasn't too worried about it, either. A lot of praying had gone into this visit, and I knew I wouldn't be handling it on my own.

When my cousin Cindy answered my knock, it was like a blast to the past. I was face to face with a younger, healthier Aunt Shannon. Same skinny body, same fried blonde hair, same ashtray breath.

"Just so you know," she said, "I was against this idea."

Same nasty attitude.

I followed her into the living room and found that time hadn't done much to improve the house. The dim light didn't hide the newspapers, magazines, and dirty dishes scattered everywhere, and it didn't cover up the moldy smell. A few things were different, though. No kids were running around. And no cats that I could see.

"Come on in, Gracene, and have a seat."

My eyes hadn't adjusted to the shadows, but I recognized Aunt Shannon's voice, weak as it was. When I finally did make out her figure half reclining on a couch across the room, I wasn't prepared for what I saw. She'd been scrawny the last time we met, but now she was more carcass than living, breathing human. She was propped up on pillows and hooked to oxygen by a tube that ran from a tank to her nose. And something strange—in early January, a fan was blowing directly on her.

The soles of my shoes kind of stuck to the carpet as I walked to a grungy recliner. I removed some magazines from the chair and sat down. Cindy took a seat on the couch at her mother's feet.

"Sorry to hear about your run-in with Del," Aunt Shannon said. Her voice was almost drowned out by the whirr of the fan. "But it looks like you're doing okay." She moaned and rearranged herself on the couch. "A lot better'n me."

I nodded and didn't bother to explain my so-called "run-in" had been more of a close call with death.

The oxygen tank started hissing. Cindy walked over to it and fiddled with the tube. "Mama's got end-stage COPD," she said.

"Did you catch that, Gracene?" Aunt Shannon spoke in a flat, tired voice. "*COPD* as in lung disease. And *end-stage* as in that's all, folks. As in death sentence. And I've got something to say before I go." Like she was moving in slow motion, she pushed bony fingers into the pocket of her robe and brought something out. "Got a gift for you," she said, stretching her hand toward me.

I couldn't imagine what she was holding. The last gift she ever gave me was a pair of underwear when I turned twelve. I had a pretty good hunch it wasn't undies she'd pulled from her pocket.

I walked over to her, and she pressed a gold ring with a ruby stone into my palm.

"Where ... how ...?"

Aunt Shannon looked at me with dull gray eyes. "You're mama's never coming back, Gracene, and you're never gonna find her. She's dead."

A cannon fired in my head. When the fallout settled, the only thing left standing was the answer to my question. The answer I'd suspected but not wanted. The answer I couldn't run from anymore. I made my way back to the recliner on wobbly legs and sank into the dirty seat cushion.

If Aunt Shannon had any notion of how shaken I was, she didn't show it. She straightened her hunched shoulders as much as possible and cleared her throat like she was about to deliver a speech she'd been rehearsing.

"Don't know if you remember or not that Del and your mama fought all the time. I suspect it was because Del had the hots for her and she couldn't stand the sight of him. To get even with her, he picked on you." A weak chuckle came from Aunt Shannon's throat. "Whenever she caught him at it, she'd lay into him something fierce. That was always quite a sight— little bitty Shirley charging at Del like a mama bear protecting her cub. He couldn't do nothin' except cover his face ... or his private parts."

She shut her eyes for a few seconds like she'd fallen asleep, but then she opened them halfway. "Your mama couldn't watch out for you twenty-four seven. She was desperate to move out of my house and get you away from Del, but she didn't make enough money for you two to live on your own. She begged me to send him packing, but, to tell the truth, I was half scared of him." Aunt Shannon twisted her ashy face into a scowl. "He was a nasty excuse for a human being. Even if I'd told him to go, he wouldn't of left 'til he was good and ready."

I opened my hand and gazed at the ring resting in my palm. I remembered Mama and Del's fights, but I'd never known they'd been about me.

"Anyway," Aunt Shannon said, "real late one night after all you kids had gone to bed, I heard screams. There were just a few, and they stopped sudden like, so I figured they must've come from an animal out in the woods." She nodded toward the window. "I heard sounds like that all the time. But the next thing I knew, Del came into the living room pale and wild-eyed and told me there'd been an accident and he needed my help."

When Aunt Shannon rubbed her temples, I couldn't help but notice the way the blackish-blue veins showed through the papery skin of her hands.

"He claimed Shirley had come home late from work and caught him outside your window, 'playing a trick' on you. She flew at him in a rage, and when he tried to push her away, he must've shoved too hard. She fell and hit her head on a rock. When she didn't move, he checked on her and she was dead."

Aunt Shannon paused and eyed me from behind droopy lids. "You okay? Want me to stop?"

My heart felt like it was pressed in a vise, and I thought I was going to be sick. For so many years I'd hidden the truth about my mother from myself. Now that it was out in the open, I didn't know if I could stand it. But I took a deep breath and shook my head.

"Anyway, that was his story," Aunt Shannon continued. "He was in a panic and wanted me to help him hide the body. When I refused and said we should call the police, he went ballistic. Flew into a rage and insisted that with his rap sheet no one would believe it was an accident. Said if we reported this, he'd be as good as dead." Her chin began to tremble. "He threatened me. Said if he was gonna be accused of one death, another wouldn't make much difference."

She reached up and adjusted the nosepiece to the oxygen tube. Then she took a few shallow breaths. "The night was so hot that steam was rising off the pond, and there wasn't a whiff of air. I could hear frogs croaking, and that clicking sound cicadas make was about to drive me mad."

A shiver went through me as she described every detail of my dream.

"Del went to my storage shed to get some old blankets." She pointed a shaky finger at the ring in my hand. "While he was gone, I took that off Shirley. She'd always prized it, and I wanted something good to remember her by. When Del brought the blankets, we wrapped her body in them."

A wheezing fit attacked Aunt Shannon, and Cindy grabbed an inhaler from a box on the coffee table. She shook it and handed it to her mother, who clutched the inhaler like it was a rope thrown to a drowning woman. While she held it in her mouth and breathed, Cindy left and came back with a glass of water. Aunt Shannon took a sip, then laid her head back and closed her eyes.

"That's enough for today," Cindy said in the bossy tone she'd used since she was a kid.

"No! She can't stop now." I balled my hands into fists. I'd come this far. No way was I leaving without knowing the whole story.

"I'm okay," Aunt Shannon said. "It's been twenty-two years. This is ending today." With a lot of whimpering, she shifted higher onto her pillows. "Del tied the blankets around Shirley with rope and wire he found in the shed. Then, after he loaded her body into an old boat I had, he tied some rocks to her. He rowed to the middle of the pond, while I watched from the bank."

From the beginning, Aunt Shannon had told her story with all the emotion of a news reporter. But at that point, she hugged herself tight and began to rock back and forth. Her voice trembled as she spoke. "When I heard the splash of Shirley's body hitting the water, I felt like I was the one being buried. I could feel the water on my skin and my body growing colder as I sunk deeper and deeper ..." She covered her face with her hands. At first, sniffs came from behind them and then wails. Between her cries, she whined, "I should've fought him. Should've turned him in. But if I was dead, what would happen to my kids? And to you, Gracene? Who'd look after you?"

She took the tissue Cindy offered and wiped her eyes. After she'd composed herself a little, she raised herself up and looked at me. "Del left town that night, and I never saw or heard from him until a few months ago. Right before you got out of prison."

I nodded, remembering what she'd told me at Kate's.

"In the months after we buried Shirley, it was all I could do to hold myself together. Every day I worried you or one of my kids would find out what happened. I'd try to sleep but kept having nightmares about body parts floating to the top of the pond. One summer we had a bad drought, and the lower the pond water got, the closer I came to losing my mind." She gave me a hard stare. "And questions. You were so nosy, Gracene. Always hounding me with so many questions. I had to cover up one lie with another, and I figured it was just a matter of time till I got caught in them or let something slip. And I figured the older you got the more you'd go snooping around for answers."

"That's why you couldn't wait to get rid of me," I said. "Why you never lifted a finger to get me out of trouble, even when I was a kid."

"I should've treated you better, I know that. But the sooner you got away from my place, the safer we'd all be." Her chest rattled as she gasped for air. "But I'm tired. Tired of being scared. Tired of hiding the truth. I'm calling the police tomorrow and telling them everything. If Del was lying about it being an accident, maybe a body—or what's left of one—will give an answer. And maybe Shirley can finally get the resting place she deserves."

Aunt Shannon collapsed against the pillows again and closed her eyes, like telling this story had sucked out her last drop of life.

"It's time for you to go, Gracene," Cindy said.

I walked to the door and let myself out.

CHAPTER EIGHTEEN

mercurial—*changeable; volatile; erratic*
reverent—*deeply respectful*
sanctify—*to make holy; to purify from sin*

ME AND REGINA STOOD IN ICY DRIZZLE AND WATCHED PEOPLE
inside a circle of crime-scene tape carry out their grisly task.
They were officers from the Logan County Sheriff's Department
and agents and crime scene analysts from the Oklahoma State
Bureau of Investigation.

True to her word, Aunt Shannon told her story to the police.
Now at the end of January, the work of finding Mama's remains
was about to begin. Yesterday, irrigation pumps had been
brought in to drain the pond. Today, a crusty layer of ice covered
a slate-gray mud hole.

Men wearing heavy blue jackets, stocking hats, water-proof
gloves, and waders were preparing to plod through the muck.
They'd be searching for bits and pieces of my mother's bones that
by now were scattered all over the bottom of the pond and probably in the land around it. Other workers were setting up
contraptions of wood and screen for sifting through all that goo.

I didn't envy them. They all whispered as they worked, and their faces had somber expressions like the ones people wear at funerals. I guess that in a way, the workers *were* at a gravesite.

I clenched my jaw to keep my teeth from chattering both from the cold and from nerves.

Regina took hold of my gloved hand. "You okay?"

"Uh-huh."

She raised an eyebrow. "You sure?"

I shrugged. I wasn't sure about a lot of things. Sometimes, I'd be at peace knowing Mama had loved me—had loved me so much she'd died trying to protect me. Other times, it was all I could do to get out of bed and go through the motions of living. But in spite of my mercurial moods, deep inside I knew God would carry me through.

I reached my hand under my wool scarf and fingered the ruby ring, hanging on a chain around my neck. Ever since I'd learned Mama hadn't deserted me, memories had come flooding back. Good memories that had been buried deep under years of hate.

"I remember walking through these woods with Mama one spring when I was four or five," I said. "We made crowns out of vines and flowers and pretended we were fairies." I swiped at the tears about to freeze on my face. "Can you picture me as a fairy?"

Regina gave a quick laugh. "Of course, I can. There's not a little girl alive who hasn't pretended to be a fairy at least once in her life."

I thought more about that day and the smile Mama had been wearing. It was the same one as in my birthday photo. I'd studied that picture at least a thousand times over the years and had searched so hard for the sadness or fear behind the smile that I'd completely missed the joy and pride and love in it.

My breath came out in stream of smoke, as I looked all around me and sighed. "This pond isn't so bad in warm weather. Part of me just wants to let Mama stay where she is. I could put up a nice marker and let her rest in peace here."

"Not a bad idea," Regina said. "Unfortunately, that decision isn't up to you. And who knows? Maybe even after all these years, they'll find some evidence that tells whether this was an accident or a murder."

I pulled my scarf tighter around my neck. "I don't know if I care."

She turned to face me. "Does that mean you've forgiven Del?"

I shook my head hard. "No way. But with or without a murder conviction, Del will probably leave prison feet first. And he's already in hell ... one he made for himself. I don't know that anything worse could happen to him."

The sheriff walked over to us and removed his hat. "Mornin' ladies. We're about to get started here." He spoke in a reverent voice, like he was in church. "But it'll be slow-going, and it's threatening rain again. Why don't you go home? I promise I'll call you the minute we find anything."

I thanked him, and me and Regina walked toward her van. It had been raining off and on for three days, and the ground squished under our feet.

We got in the van, and Regina cranked up the heater and defroster. When the windshield cleared, we crunched along the gravel drive of Aunt Shannon's property. Two weeks ago, I went back to see Aunt Shannon and told her I forgave her. It wasn't easy, and I'm not sure it was totally sincere. But she was dying, and it seemed like the right thing to do. She passed away three days later, so maybe it was. And maybe at some point my forgiveness will be genuine.

After Aunt Shannon's confession, I'd sometimes think of how my life might've been different if I'd known the truth sooner. I'd think of those wasted years—of never belonging anywhere, of believing I wasn't good enough for even my own mama to love me, of hating everyone, especially myself. And when I thought of the child who missed the chance at life, my anger would threaten to rise like a zombie and suck from me all the joy and peace of my new faith. But I found a way of coping. The old Gracene managed her anger with counting and breathing. The new one was discovering praying and singing worked a lot better.

Regina reached the end of the drive and came to a stop before turning. I twisted in my seat and peered through the frosty back window of the van at the pond, the shed, and the woods. They looked like hazy images in a dream ... or a nightmare.

Aunt Shannon left this place to her kids. Her ashes hardly had time to cool before they put it up for sale. Mama's remains would soon be moved, and there was no reason for me to come here again. Ever. I raised my hand and waved good-bye—not to my past but to the pain and anger and guilt that had kept me from rising above it.

Me and Regina rode for a while without saying a word. Finally, I broke the silence. "Do you think I'm terrible?"

She frowned. "What are you talking about?"

"Because I can't forgive Del. Do you think I'm awful?"

"No, Gracene, I don't think you're awful. I think you're human. And I'm still marveling that you forgave Shannon. That couldn't have been easy."

"It wasn't. And I'm still working on it. I've been praying about it, but ... I'm not perfect."

She shook her head. "No, you're not. I'm not. None of us are. That's why we're thankful for sanctifying grace."

"Sanctifying grace?"

"Yeah. Some people call it perfecting grace. When we turn over our lives to God, that doesn't make us perfect—at least not in this lifetime. The Christian journey is a process, and we're going to struggle. But we have the desire to please God, and he sends his Spirit to help us. And, because of what Jesus did for us, on the day we're finally in the Father's presence, we will be perfect." She glanced in her rearview mirror and changed lanes. "Does that make sense?"

"Sort of. I'll have to study on it." I chewed on my thumbnail. "Or maybe I'll ask Hallie."

Me and Regina both laughed.

I raised my hand and counted on my fingers. "Prevenient, justifying, sanctifying ... any other graces I should know about?"

Regina was silent for a minute. She squinted her eyes like she was thinking hard. "Well, I'm no Bible scholar, but the way I understand it, there's only one grace—the undeserved and unearned love of God. You're right, though. Those are three ways it manifests itself and empowers us to become more and more like Christ."

The drizzle was turning into rain that hit against the van with loud splats.

I leaned my head against the cool glass of the passenger window. "Man, I've got a lot to learn about being a Christian."

Regina adjusted the speed of the wipers, and they slapped across the windshield with a steady beat.

"We all do, Gracene. We all do."

Cardboard boxes crammed with my stuff were scattered all over the apartment. It was almost midnight, and me and Hallie were buzzing around like worker bees, trying to get me packed up. Six short months ago, I'd moved into Transformation Place with everything I owned either on my back or in a paper sack. Now it would take these boxes and at least two trips with a pickup to move me out. Chase would provide the pickup, and him and Sean would provide the muscle to load and unload it.

Of course, a lot of what I was taking came from Transformation Place.

"That's the deal, Gracene," Regina had said earlier that evening at my graduation party. "You held up your end of the bargain, and we're holding up ours. You have furnishings and furniture—everything you need to start life on your own."

Did I, I thought. *Everything?* Funny, I'd had plenty of doubts about coming to Transformation Place, and I had almost as many about leaving it. Thinking about survival in the "real" world was disturbing a lot of my new-found peace. But I had a strong support system: good friends, good job, a Christian therapist, and —most important—my faith. And there was something else working in my favor.

Two weeks ago, Hallie's parents called her. They'd been praying, they said, and doing some soul-searching. They wanted to mend the broken ties with their daughter. Hallie was cautious. She'd been doing a lot of praying, too, but she was struggling to overcome her own pain of being rejected. She explained her reluctance to them and asked for their patience. She also made it perfectly clear she would never move back to their farm.

So in a month—when her stay at Transformation Place was complete—she'd be joining me in my apartment. I figured it wouldn't be long before her and Sean got married and she'd be moving out again. In the meantime, I could keep depending on her friendship and Bible lessons to get me through shaky moments. And because my new apartment was so close to Transformation Place, I could depend on Regina, too.

Hallie came into the kitchen where I was packing dishes. She was wearing her wrinkled gown and the fuzzy blue socks I'd given her for Christmas.

"If you and Sean end up getting married," I said, "I'm buying you some new lingerie."

She giggled and blushed pinker than the roses on her gown. "Behave yourself, Gracene," she scolded. But I noticed she didn't deny the possibility of marriage.

As for me and Chase, we were at that "close friends" stage. But it was a friendship that was getting stronger every day, and it gave me hope that maybe it would grow into something more. I prayed that he'd been sincere at the Christmas party about being "more into grace," if the time ever came when I should tell him about my abortion.

Me and Hallie worked, dividing the dishes into hers and mine. "You go ahead and take that," she said about the tea pitcher I was holding up. "I can get another one." She sighed as she wrapped a dish towel around some silverware. "I thank God every day, Gracene, for the miracle that brought us together."

I grinned as I moved from sorting dishes to sorting canned goods. The subject of miracles was an on-going discussion between us. "Hallie, you think everything's a miracle. A raise in pay, a cleared-up zit, a sunrise—they're all miracles to you."

"Well, what do you consider a miracle?" she asked.

"I don't know. But for sure not something that's cured by face cream. A miracle should involve something supernatural, something that can't be explained by science or coincidence. Like God talking to people in an actual voice or Jesus walking on water."

"So you believe the miracles in the Bible actually happened?"

I placed a can of peaches into a box. "Yeah, sure. But I don't believe God performs those kinds of miracles anymore."

Hallie gave me a fake frown and shook her finger at me."Oh, ye of little faith."

I was never going to convince her that perfectly normal situations weren't miracles and that these days God was no longer in the miracle business. So I kept quiet and let her cling to her fantasy.

We worked until we had the kitchen and living room packed up. Then I tackled my bedroom.

I was cleaning out my closet, when my fingers touched cool, smooth metal under a stack of T-shirts on the overhead shelf. Right away I knew what it was.

"Hey, Hallie," I called in a timid voice. "C'mere a sec." When she appeared in the doorway, I held the wind chime toward her. Its kinked, twisted strings kept the tubes and pieces of glass from making anything but dull clanks. "Want this?" I raised my eyebrows in a kind of plea for forgiveness.

Her eyes opened wide. After a moment, she started giggling, and then her giggles turned into belly laughs.

We both collapsed onto my bed. I held the chime against my chest, as we rolled side to side and howled with laughter.

"Oh my gosh, Gracene," she said between gasps. "If you only knew how hard I searched for that. I was sooo mad at you. If I'd had enough money, I would've bought a dozen chimes and strung them up all over the apartment."

I sat on the edge of the bed and scooted the chime toward her. "Well, here's this one. You can start with it."

She raised up and straightened her gown over her knobby knees. "No, thanks. I have the chime you gave me, and I like its happy little click-clacks a lot better."

She frowned at the chime on the bed and shoved it back at me before she started toward the door.

As she walked away, a thought—triggered by all the wind chime talk—came to me. "I guess I do believe in miracles," I said. "In a way."

She turned around with a satisfied look on her face. "Oh really?"

"Yeah. I believe miracles can happen inside of people. Like on the night Del attacked me and I was sure I was a goner. And then I heard you tap on the chime and say you were going for help and—"

"What are you talking about?" Hallie scrunched up her forehead.

"You know. I told you about that. I'm sure I did." I thought back. "Or maybe it was Regina. Anyway, the sound of the chime and your message gave me the will to hang on and to fight." I smiled. "I'll admit *that* was a miracle."

Hallie walked to the bed and sank down beside me. She twisted her hands in her lap and studied them. "I don't know what you're saying, Gracene. All I could think of that night was running for help. I'm sure there are a lot of details I don't remember, but I'm absolutely certain about this." She faced me, and her blue eyes were as big as silver dollars. "I didn't say a word. And I never tapped that chime."

AUTHOR'S NOTE

Dear Readers,

In 2008, I became acquainted with a few of the residents and workers of Exodus House in Oklahoma City. Exodus House is part of the prisoner re-entry program sponsored by the Criminal Justice and Mercies Ministry Oklahoma Annual Conference of the United Methodist Church. Until I became aware of this program, I had never considered the difficulties ex-prisoners face in trying to piece their lives back together. I was dumbstruck at the challenges: finding an affordable place to live with a supportive environment, getting a job while having a criminal record, overcoming mountains of debt which have accumulated from unreasonable fines and jail and court costs. Day-to-day operations become big problems when a person doesn't have transportation to get to a job or money for bus passes or a drivers license. Even getting decent work clothes can be difficult. Add to this list concerns over child custody or dealing with addictions or health issues, and it is no wonder that in Oklahoma the prisoner recidivism rate—without additional support—is almost one in three. This book is a work of fiction, but in it I've tried to present some very real issues in a sympathetic and entertaining way. I hope it will entice people to read about and perhaps actively respond to them.

Equally important, I've tried to demonstrate the impact faith can have in overcoming impossible odds. Coincidentally (or perhaps not), about the time I became acquainted with Exodus House, my pastor began preaching a series of sermons on grace. I had already been thinking of writing a novel inspired by Exodus House, and when I began deeply considering the concept of grace, the idea for my character Gracene and her faith journey was born. Hopefully, this book can be used to bring about social awareness and, at the same time, spread the message of God's matchless gift of grace made available through his Son, Jesus.

If you would like to learn more about CJAMM and Exodus House, please visit their website: http://okumcministries.org/CJAMM/Exodus_House.htm. Also, a book lives or dies by its reviews. If you enjoyed this book and would like to help spread the word about prison ministry and God's grace, please recommend it to your friends and/or leave a review. I would be forever grateful!

Sincerely,

Dee Dee Chumley

PS Please visit www.deedeechumley.com for recipes of some of Flo's down-home dishes.

ACKNOWLEDGMENTS

Any writer who has ever put her name on the cover of a book surely must have experienced a twinge of guilt, as a good story is seldom the product of the author alone. Many friends and professionals contributed to the writing and publishing of *Some Form of Grace*, and I am grateful for the opportunity to recognize them here. First, I want to thank Robin Wertz, Resident Supervisor at Exodus House in Oklahoma City. Without her willingness to share her story, this book would never have been started much less finished. Appreciation also goes to Dr. Adrian Cole for his series of sermons on God's amazing and abundant grace. (Yes, I was listening, AC!) Gene Christian, retired District Attorney for District 6 in Oklahoma, gave me excellent legal and crime scene information, and Kate McDaniel, BSN, RN, CCRN, made sure my description of COPD symptoms and treatment was accurate. She is also one of the first readers to encourage me to pursue publication. Among my other astute and knowledgeable beta readers: Gladys Fink, my mother (whom I can always trust to say good things about my writing); Brenda Price, retired librarian and Board Certified Teacher; Nancy McKinnis, avid reader, fellow book club member, and devoted friend; Cheryl Devoe, retired English teacher extraordinaire, who not only read my book but also developed insightful and thought-provoking questions for the Discussion Guide available on my website. Amanda Bird of The Book Nest Literary Services, polished my content and grammar. An enthusiastic shout-out goes to the Inklings, my multi-talented and long-suffering critique group. Their input, advice, and encouragement make me appear a far better writer than I really am. Brandi Barnett, Martha Bryant, Kelly Bristow, Sonia Gensler, Lisa Marotta, and Mari Farthing, there aren't enough words to express my gratitude. Last but certainly not least, thank you, Bill, for your patience and encouragement in my writing journey and for being my Twitter coach!